MIND GAMES

A Novel by

STEVIE TURNER

OTHER WORKS BY STEVIE TURNER

CONTENTS

CHAPTER 1

FRANCES

She could not bear the sight of him. As he brought the car to a halt outside the familiar end-of-terrace house, Frances Andrews jerked the passenger door open and jumped out, slamming it behind her with more force than was really necessary. She glared at her husband Martin over the car's roof, as he slowly unfolded his 6 foot 2 inch frame from the driver's seat.

"What's the point of coming back here? We're getting nowhere!"

Martin, pale and tight-lipped, activated the car's central locking system with a click of his key fob.

"This time it's my idea, so humour me if you can."

Even the sound of his voice grated on her nerves. Frances turned around sharply and headed past Rhona's obviously new Honda Civic, which sat squarely on a concrete pad in what had been a pretty front garden 18 months before. She ignored Martin as he rang the bell, and took another quick glance at the counsellor's car over her shoulder.

"Business must be booming."

She heard Martin sigh beside her.

"Yeah, I expect Ipswich is full of shitbags like me beating a path to her door. Probably that's why out-of-towners call it Ip-*shit*."

"You're in the right place then."

She shot a thin smile towards Rhona Perkins, purple haired and still resembling a middle-aged hippie, who greeted them with what seemed to Frances like genuine warmth.

"Frances! Martin! Lovely to see you again! *Do* come in!"

"Hello Rhona." Frances stepped into the hallway as the counsellor closed the door behind them. "Thanks for fitting us in at such short notice."

"No problem." Rhona ushered them along a passageway with one hand. "First on the left as usual; make yourselves comfortable."

The consulting room was almost as she remembered, with the blue velvet two-seater sofa and matching armchair opposite, but a newer looking Persian rug than previously and even more shelves of books lining the walls. Chaz, the same sleepy ginger cat, stretched out languidly on the window sill in the late evening sun. A fresh vase of flowers and three glasses of water were on a glass coffee table placed in-between the sofa and armchair, along with the compulsory box of half empty tissues.

Frances sat down carefully on the sofa, as far away from Martin as she could get. Rhona plonked herself down in the armchair and picked up her sheaf of notes.

"How long has it been since I saw you both?"

"Must be about eighteen months." Martin cleared his throat before continuing. "But it's my idea to come here this time."

Frances shrugged and crossed her legs.

"For what good it will do."

"I'm trying." Martin sighed. "At least I'm here of my own accord this time."

"Glad to hear it!" Rhona chuckled and looked up from her notes. "So; what brings the two of you here today?"

"Same old problem." Frances rolled her eyes to the ceiling. "Little did I know that thirty five years ago I married the bloody Porn Baron of Norfolk."

She was aware that Martin had shifted uncomfortably in his seat. Rhona nodded and wrote quickly in a notepad.

"And how has this affected you?"

"There's no trust." Frances sighed. "Time and time again he's lied to me and told me he's stopped looking at it, but then I catch him out. He has a terrible addiction that has ruined us. It's caused him to have affairs and sex with prostitutes, and in the past I've even found a hidden camera in our bedroom. For all I know my naked body could be all over the web by now!"

Rhona nodded sagely before turning her gaze to Martin.

"And Martin, do you wish to add anything to your wife's statement?"

Frances heard her husband's ritual throat-clearing and wanted to scream.

"It seems she's made up her mind to leave. Coming here is a last resort. I really have stopped looking at it now, but she doesn't believe me."

"I wonder why?" Frances replied with more than a touch of irony.

"I always tell my couples that a marriage needs to be built on a foundation of love and trust." Rhona took a sip from her glass. "Without these any marriage will founder."

"I don't love him anymore, let alone trust him." Frances wiped away a tear. "I've had enough."

She felt relieved to state out loud what had been on her mind for some time, and was aware Martin's shoulders had sagged with the disappointment of her revelation. Frances felt the awkwardness of a momentary silence, broken only by Rhona's quietly confident tones.

"Frances, what would you like to get out of these sessions?"

With Rhona's eyes on her and Martin waiting expectantly for an answer, Frances decided to disillusion the two of them even more.

"Nothing. I'm only here because Martin begged me. I don't expect to gain anything from coming here. Whatever I felt for my husband died a long time ago. All we do now is play mind games with each other. He hides a porn stash, and I can't rest until I've found it."

She could see that Rhona's face had remained expressionless as the counsellor nodded and turned towards Martin. Frances sighed, sat back, crossed her arms, and looked at the floor.

"Martin, can I ask you the same question please?"

Frances made a point of not turning her head towards her husband as he shrugged and fiddled with the cuff of his shirt.

"Just to get my marriage on more of an even footing and for my wife not to move out would be a start. I'm not after miracles, as you can tell."

Frances looked up as the counsellor wrote furiously, her pen sweeping across the page in broad strokes. She listened as Rhona talked and jotted down notes at the same time.

"We covered a lot of ground at your last visit. If you remember we talked about how we lay the foundation stones for a happy marriage, about communication, and about giving each other space and privacy. I think a good place to start with today is when you think it all went wrong. Frances, would you like to start this time? Martin, you will get your chance to speak at our next meeting. Is this okay with both of you?"

"Yeah, it's okay with me." Martin replied with a weary air.

"Frances?"

Frances nodded while casting her mind back 35 years to the first sign that with hindsight she should have taken more notice of. She felt like kicking herself in anger. She was so stupidly in love that the importance of what had happened to her that night had failed to register even one warning bell in her head.

CHAPTER 2

As she lay wide awake on her back listening to her new husband's even breathing, Frances wished she'd taken the plunge years before and lost her virginity at the same time as her little clique of girlfriends in the sixth form were losing theirs. As far as she could tell, saving herself for her wedding night, especially if the bridegroom was a virgin like Martin, could only lead to a kind of all-pervading disappointment that was still almost palpable in the room, two hours after the painful fumbling fiasco was over.

She turned on her side and sighed. Streaks of moonlight illuminated the pearly buttons on the bodice of her wedding dress as it hung from the doorframe in front of her. She shifted about so as to avoid a definite wet patch between them in the bed, and hoped the tell-tale evidence of their lovemaking was dry enough by the time the chambermaid came in to clean.

She must have dozed, because the next thing she knew she was coming back to consciousness feeling chilled to the bone. What she had sensed was daylight through her closed eyelids was actually the soft glow from a bedside lamp. She could hear heavy breathing and occasionally a kind of animalistic grunt. Opening her eyes a little she noticed a clock on the wall opposite showing 03:25. Something had woken her up.

The November winds whistled through cracks in the hotel's old sash windows. Wide awake now, she soon discovered the reason why she was so cold. Sitting up slightly, she was aware that Martin was on his knees and had pulled back the blankets. Her naked body had been exposed, and she saw her new husband masturbating and gazing down at her with a kind of enraptured awe, lost in a world of his own. In the split second before her consciousness registered with him, she had a distinct uneasy moment and quickly pulled the covers up around her shoulders as Martin hastily jumped back into bed beside her.

"What are you doing?"

Her voice sounded higher than normal, and suddenly she wished she'd brought a nightdress.

"I thought you were awake. Sorry."

The lie was blatant, but it was not the time or the place to start an argument. She turned over on her side again away from him, and held on to the blankets with one hand.

"No I wasn't. Don't ever do that again."

"Of course not. Sorry."

She lay awake for the remainder of the night wondering how to broach the subject again in the morning. Was it normal for a man to want to do something like that? Did all men do this when their wives were asleep? Frances had not the foggiest idea, and there was nobody she knew well enough to ask. Her parents were old-fashioned and rather strait-laced, and she had no older, more experienced sister. She would have died with embarrassment relating the tale to any of her girlfriends, and therefore resigned herself to the fact that it was just an aberration. By morning Martin was his usual loving self, and what had happened in the small hours was never mentioned again.

***

"So, Frances…" Rhona looked up from her notes and smiled. "Did the episode cause you any long-term concerns?

Frances decided it was time to tell the truth whether Martin liked what he heard or not.

"I thought about it often over the following months, as to me it had seemed a strange thing for a person to do. Perhaps my parents had brought me up too conservatively, but to me it just seemed…I don't know…*kinky*." She nodded. "Yes, kinky is the word. I don't think women forget something like that, but eventually when it didn't happen again I put it to the back of my mind."

"And you carried on having a normal sexual relationship?" Rhona sat back in her chair and focused her gaze on Frances.

"Yes. It all seemed fine for a few years until our first son Colin was born."

"What happened then?"

Frances took a sideways glance at Martin, who continued fiddling with his shirt cuff and staring at the floor.

"I was hoovering the living room carpet one day, and stuck the nozzle thing under a gap between our display unit and the floor. I felt it hit something under there, and so I turned off the hoover and got down on my hands and knees and fished about. I pulled out two porn videos. We'd only just had a party a couple of days before. We were leaving London to move to the countryside. I tried to pass them off at first as something one of the partygoers might have left there for a joke, but of course when I'd thought about it a little bit more, it occurred to me that they probably belonged to Martin ."

"Did you tackle him about it?" Rhona nodded sagely.

"Yes." Frances sighed. "I was shocked. He told me it was harmless fun and that a workmate had lent them to him. He said he'd take them back again the next day."

"How did you feel about porn being in the house?"

"I hated it. I told Martin to take the videos outside and put them in his van. It was after that I started checking in nooks and crannies in case there were any more hanging about. When I didn't find anything, again I tended to forget after a few months, but something else was waiting round the corner which would turn out to be the most embarrassing moment in my entire life."

She looked at Martin with venom, whose gaze stayed rooted to the carpet.

CHAPTER 3

She wondered if it had been a disaster moving from Woodmansterne to the kind of Norfolk village where everyone knew everybody else. As far as the locals were concerned, they were 'those Londoners' and therefore outsiders. Cosy conversations would cease as soon as they walked into the Ten Bells public house, or into the village hall which doubled as a sub post office and café on Tuesdays and Thursdays. Stuck at home with a toddler while Martin was out at work, Frances felt isolated and in need of friendship.

The answer came to her early one morning in that dream-like state between sleeping and waking. She would host mother and baby get-togethers once a week in her front room. Her son would get to know the local children, and their mothers would see that clearly she was not some hoity-toity Londoner with square plates, Jesus-creeper sandals and designer clothes, but an ordinary woman just like themselves who was lonely and eager to forge new friendships.

She pretended not to notice the post office assistant scrutinising the advert, and decided to force herself to buy a cup of coffee and stay awhile in the hope that somebody might show an interest. Colin had found a toy car to whizz around the hall, and Frances pretended not to notice that all the local women had gathered together on the one other table, laughing, chattering and dangling babies or toddlers on their hips. Taking her courage in both hands, she stood up and went over to them.

"Hi. I'm Frances. I've not long moved to this area, and I've just put an advert on the notice board over there about a mother and baby group I'm setting up at my home on Monday mornings. Would any of you like to come along? I'm at number four Elm View. It's on the new estate."

She did her best to ignore several mothers looking at her as though she had grown two heads, and continued to smile inanely at the group.

"I'm at number sixteen." A mother spoke whilst rocking a newborn in the crook of one arm. "That sounds like a good idea. I've only been here a year or so myself. I'm Diane."

"Pleased to meet you." Frances heaved a sigh of relief. "Come round about ten o'clock. Bring some friends; the more the merrier."

"Will do." Diane nodded. "Where are you from?"

"Woodmansterne, on the outskirts of London. My husband Martin works for a new company based near Norwich, he's an electrician."

"Our house needs a total re-wire." Another woman in the group picked up a screaming toddler from the floor. "You should send him round. We're next door to the Ten Bells."

"Sure." Frances wasn't sure if she had heard right. "He's happy to give free estimates."

"Cheers. I'm Sue. I'll come round to yours on Monday with Diane."

"Great!"

She came away from the hall feeling quite elated.

***

She had the kettle boiling and the biscuits heaped tastefully on plates. A little after ten o'clock the doorbell rang, and Frances was surprised to find that seven other women had decided to join Diane and Sue. Soon her front room was alive with the sound of babies crying, toddlers fighting, and mothers gossiping over the hubbub. She ran back and forth making cups of tea and coffee in-between chatting, happy in the knowledge that she was slowly getting to know the local women whom she discovered were not daft in the head after all.

Towards lunch time some of the toddlers appeared fractious, although their somewhat talkative mothers seemed in no hurry to leave. Frances found a tape of an old children's programme which Colin had liked to watch. She had written 'Disney' in capital letters on the label some time ago, and knew the short film would subdue the children in no time at all. She inserted the video into the player, and turned on the TV. Immediately the toddlers quietened down and sat on the carpet together. She remembered the video lasted about 30 minutes; just enough time to collect all the crockery, load the dishwasher, and then send the mothers on their way.

As she turned away from the TV and began to gather up cups and plates, all talk suddenly ceased in the room. She looked up to find that every woman was gazing fixedly at the screen, horrified. The sound of her own voice moaning in pleasure was all-pervading in the room, and for a brief stunned moment she stood and watched herself, naked as the day she was born, spreading her knees and lifting them up, exposing her perineum ready for Martin to perform oral sex.

The first titter jolted her out of her stupor. The cup and plate in her hand dropped to the floor in her efforts to reach the video player. The toddlers were looking at the screen unconcerned, as though it was an everyday occurrence to watch couples performing cunnilingus. With her face burning in embarrassment, she bashed her palm against the off switch. Immediately the toddlers began to complain at the interruption, but were hastily grabbed by their mothers and bundled out of the door. Frances suddenly found herself alone in a room filled with the detritus of the morning; biscuit crumbs had been ground into the carpet, tea had been spilt on the settee, a baby had posseted on one of her best velvet cushions, and now the whole village would find out in the blink of an eye that she obviously gained great satisfaction from oral sex.

***

"So you see…by watching myself on the TV screen I was in no doubt that Martin had hidden a camera somewhere in our bedroom. I wanted to *kill* him at the time! Can you imagine all your neighbours finding out the deepest secrets of your love life? In the end we had to move a few miles away when the sniggering became too much."

Frances shuddered at remembering the feelings of violation, especially the walk of shame the next day to the village supermarket.

"I told you I was sorry." Martin sighed. "I took the camera down straight away. You watched me do it."

"Yes, but are there any more?" Frances looked at him in disgust. "Even now I'm still never quite sure if I'm being filmed sitting on the toilet! You say you love me, but you filmed me without my consent. What kind of relationship is that?"

"Martin, you will have your turn to speak at our next session." Rhona interjected. "I work better if I can concentrate on one partner at a time."

"Sorry." Martin shrugged. "Sorry for being alive, really. I'm the biggest shitbag ever to walk this earth."

"Too bloody right you are." Frances tossed her light brown hair. "The sooner we can get divorced, the better as far as I'm concerned."

"Let's arrange some times where you do nothing else but talk to each other." Rhona jumped in to diffuse the tension. "I like to get my clients talking, *not arguing*, but calmly discussing their problems maybe twice or three times a week."

"I've got nothing to say, apart from I don't trust him." Frances sighed. "If you've been through what I've been through; the lies, the affairs, the camera and the prostitutes just for starters, you wouldn't have much else to say either."

Rhona tapped her pen on the arm of her chair.

"Good communication between couples is a must. If you decide to give it a try, let's say….half an hour every Monday, Wednesday and Friday evenings between eight and eight thirty. What do you say?"

Out of the corner of her eye Frances saw that Martin had turned towards her, waiting for her reply. She shrugged.

"It won't do much good."

"We'll see." Martin gave her hand a brief squeeze. "Let's give it a go."

"What shall we talk about?" Frances turned and gave him a stare. How's…what's new in the world of porn, or … the best place to hang around to pick up a prossie?"

"I already know where that is." Martin grinned at her facetiously.

"Yeah, I bet you do." Frances looked away from him in disgust. "You've been there often enough."

"Let's stop it here." Rhona cut in quickly and smiled. "Come and see me next week and let me know how you're getting on."

CHAPTER 4

MARTIN

"So….what do you want to talk about?"

Stretched out on the sofa in his efforts to impart a state of pseudo-nonchalance, Martin raked a hand across his greying hair and looked across at his wife sitting stiff and upright in the armchair opposite.

"How about why you continue treating me this way, the affairs, the prostitutes and the porn, while leading me to believe you've given it all up but really you're lying through your back teeth. You *know* it's the porn addiction in the first place that's led to everything else."

He watched her exhaling shakily with suppressed anger, and heaved himself up on one elbow.

"I don't think I had an addiction, but…whatever; I've definitely given up this time, but of course you don't believe me."

"I wonder why?" Frances gave a wry laugh. "Try and see things from my perspective. This must be the fifth or sixth time we've had this conversation."

Martin shrugged.

"I didn't want to give it up then, but now I do."

"Only because I'm thinking of moving out. You see lonely nights in front of you, with nobody to cook your dinner."

"I don't care if you never cook for me again." He shook his head. "Cooking is not the reason I married you. Fran, I love you. I don't want you to leave."

"I've heard it all before, time and time again." She shook her head. "We need a break from each other. Not only am I angry with you, I'm also angry at myself for being so gullible and believing you every time you told me you'd given it up. I now can't believe a word you say, and I'll never be able to trust you again."

"I didn't know about addiction at the time." Martin looked at Frances beseechingly. "I still say it wasn't an addiction, but I'm happy to go along with what you say now. I'm a changed man now. It's a question of making you believe me."

"And there our paths diverge." Frances sighed. "Or they will do as soon as I can get on the council housing list."

"You know that's not going to happen." Martin stated confidently with some degree of relief. "You're not pregnant or homeless."

"Perhaps I ought to have IVF then? A baby at fifty five isn't too uncommon these days."

Martin rolled his eyes towards the spotlights on the ceiling.

"Don't be ridiculous! All those shitty nappies and no sleep for months? We're too old for all that."

He was aware of her hostile glance in his direction.

"Who says I want *you* to be the father?"

His heart gave a sudden lurch.

"You've found somebody else?" He folded his arms to stop his hands balling into fists.

"There is somebody…yeah."

He'd had no idea. His head swam with the sure and certain knowledge that another man had made love to his wife. He wanted to tear the bastard apart.

"Who is he?"

"One of the doctors I knew when I worked at the hospital. I like him. I saw him again in Sainsbury's and we just clicked."

He looked at the new red highlights in her salt-and-pepper hair, and realised with a kind of sinking feeling that he had become too complacent and let his wife slip away.

"*I* like you." He exhaled with force. "I *love* you, for God's sake! Do I know him?"

"I'm not telling you. He's married with kids."

"So you're having an affair?" He swung his legs around to sit bolt upright opposite her."

He noticed how good his wife's legs looked; tanned and slim. He imagined them wrapped around another man's back in the height of passion, and closed his eyes momentarily against the thought.

"What's sauce for the goose is sauce for the gander. Takes one to know one and all that shit."

Gone was her good humour and placid acceptance. He realised at once that he had gone too far this time. No longer was his wife willing to accept his faults and carry on as normal. There was a new man on the scene, all due to his stubborn selfishness and absolute refusal to comply with her wishes.

"I'm so sorry, but I really have stopped now. The only problem is that you don't believe me."

Frances shrugged, then sank back against the armchair and sighed.

"I've heard it so many times that you've given up porn, but it never amounts to anything. You also seem to have a problem with authority, or at least with somebody telling you what to do, especially a woman."

"I'm really trying to change." Martin looked at her pleadingly. "I've already said that I've given up now because I *want* to. I don't know what else I can do. In time you'll see I'm a different person."

"So all my tears and distress in the past because of your affairs didn't move you one bit?" Frances shook her head. "No; it's too late. I just can't take the lies anymore. There's no trust; as soon as my back's turned you'll be at it again. I'm enjoying the fact that somebody actually finds me attractive. You've put porn first in your life for more years than I care to remember. I'm sick to death of coming in second, and realise that the only person who can put myself first is *me*."

As his wife stood up and left the room, Martin fought back tears of despair.

CHAPTER 5

He fiddled with the cuff of his shirt for something to do. He hated the thought of having to discuss his innermost feelings with a relative stranger, but it was the only way of letting his wife know how committed he was to ending the rift in his marriage. He could sense Rhona trying to make eye contact, and raised his gaze to meet hers.

"So…Martin." Rhona spoke in a soft voice. "Perhaps you'd like to tell your side of the story, and update me on how it went with your first communication sessions."

"We've only had the one." Martin replied. "But it didn't go too well."

Frances exhaled and gave her shoulders a shrug.

"That's because there's nothing left to say. I can't stand the sight of him."

"This is Martin's day." Rhona briefly glanced at Frances. "I'd like to hear what your husband wants to tell me."

"Sorry." Frances folded her arms and looked towards Martin.

"It all started long before I met Frances." Martin sighed. "My older brothers had stacks of porn magazines in their room. I was a thirteen year old kid. You can imagine how happy I was. I used to sneak into their room after school when they were out at work. By the time they'd left home and got married I was an apprentice electrician and buying my own mags."

"So the fascination with porn has carried on for…" Rhona looked back at her notes. "Forty years?"

"Yeah, something like that." Martin nodded. "It just got to be a habit I suppose."

"A habit that you now want to break?"

"I have broken it, but because I've lied to Frances in the past about stopping, she now doesn't believe me."

"And how does that make you feel?" Rhona nibbled the end of her pen before jotting down a few notes.

"Frustrated, and sad and angry with myself for not telling Fran the truth. She says I've never put her first all the time we've been married, and I realise she's right. It's always been porn. I've been a total bastard, haven't I?"

"A lack of trust breaks down the foundations of any marriage quite quickly." Rhona replied. "If both partners are willing to work hard, then trust might well be re-built over a period of time. Have you found that you've been addicted to other substances too?"

"I don't know about being addicted." Martin shrugged "I used to drink to try and feel better about myself, but found at one point that it was interfering with my ability to earn a living and be a good provider for my family, so I cut down. Now I only drink socially, so I couldn't have been addicted…could I?"

"People with addictive personalities are more likely to have more than one addiction." Rhona's face remained neutral. "However, you have proved that you *were* able to stop drinking."

"Yes, because I *wanted* to." Martin emphasised his point and looked sideways at Frances.

"*Because* we became short of money." Frances interjected with venom. "You were drinking it all away and we had two teenagers who needed new clothes every few months."

"Frances, remember how this is Martin's day?" Rhona kept her voice even. "I'll invite both of you to speak at our next session."

"Yes, I forgot." Frances held up her hands in supplication. "Sorry."

Rhona waved away the apology with one wave of her arm.

"Let's carry on. Martin … how do you feel about Frances' admitting to an affair?"

"Devastated. There's no other word for it. The one night stands I had were meaningless, even if I saw the woman again a couple of times afterwards. It was just for sex, but I know Frances must feel something deep for this guy because she's loyal to her family and it's never been in her nature to be unfaithful before. I'm just sick; sick at my own stupidity. In fact, thinking about it, I don't believe it's worth carrying on here." Martin could hear his voice faltering, and knew he was close to tears. He rammed his nails into the palms of his hands in an effort to compose himself. "Fran deserves better." He stood up and passed the car keys to Frances. "Take these. I need to get out of here."

***

As soon as he was out in the street he felt better. He had no idea where he was going, but followed the main flow of traffic up to the main road, walking without purpose or direction. When he found himself passing The Milestone public house, a familiar aroma of fermented hops lured him inside. He ordered a pint of beer, and plonked himself down on a bar stool. The temptation to drink himself into oblivion was strong, but more than ever now he wanted Frances to see that he could drink just one pint without it escalating to the whole barrel. To go home three sheets to the wind would only add fuel to the fire. He sat morosely on the bar stool and remembered how it used to be with them, whilst trying hard to cast away thoughts about who his wife's lover might possibly be.

CHAPTER 6

They were happy. Her abdomen was swollen with their first child, and if he laid behind her in bed he could not get his arms around her middle anymore. Out in the street, Martin felt proud when she walked beside him, young and radiant in her summer-yellow maternity dress and matching sun-bleached hair. He noticed how people tended to give her second glances, and some even commented on how happy she looked. She basked in their compliments. He wanted to protect her from the unwanted attention, wrap her in cotton wool, and keep her all to himself. She was his queen, and his reason for living.

When it became too uncomfortable for her to have sex, he reluctantly left her alone and turned to his old comfort – a selection of top shelf magazines which he kept under the floorboards in an untrodden corner of the front room. All he had to do when she went up to bed early was wheel the armchair out of the way, lift up the carpet and the loose floorboard, and hey presto, instant satisfaction. Afterwards, he liked to watch her sleeping, especially now that the weather was hot and her nightie remained on the chair. He knew she would hate to discover that he still did this, but luckily for him she had not caught him out a second time. He had previously brought her a see-through baby doll nightie before her pregnancy had become advanced, but had somehow not been too surprised when she had refused to wear it

***

He had given up the job at Norwich, and was living his dream of being self-employed. One of the first jobs he was asked to do was to re-wire a video rental shop. The manager, looking for ways to reduce costs, had already offered him a selection of old adult videos to keep and a cheap video player as part-payment. To be able to watch couples on TV at his own convenience was too good an opportunity to miss, and his pulse raced faster at the thought of it. He could store the videos with his magazines, and Fran was too tired and wrapped up with the coming baby to wonder why he was staying up late at night. He knew in his heart that he had already decided to take the manager up on his offer.

Three weeks before the baby was due he managed to endure a whole video on childbirth to keep in her good books, and then kissed his wife goodnight. Fifteen porn films sat underneath the armchair that his wife had just vacated, and he could not wait to retrieve them. Watching the babies go in was infinitely preferable to the sight of them coming out; the blood and guts were enough to turn his stomach. He had no idea how on earth he was going to be any use to her in the labour room.

When her time came he was surprised to find that Frances depended on him to rub away the pain in her lower back. He was glad to be able to show his strength as he worked with her to bring their baby into the world. At the first sight of his son's crowned head his eyes filled up with tears, and he knew that for as long as he lived he would fight the world to protect his wife and child from danger.

Fatherhood became a reality as Colin Martin Andrews, 8 pounds 12 ounces, and with a cry loud enough to wake the dead, entered the world at 11.45pm on 27th August 1982. Martin gazed at the swaddled bundle in his wife's arms and felt like running full-pelt along the hospital corridors just for the sheer joy of it. He was a *man*, a father, a self-employed hunter-gatherer and provider. He would turn to crime or even *kill* to ensure there was food on the table. He vowed to himself that his wife and son would never want a thing for as long as they lived.

Like a peacock showing off its feathers, he strutted home in the early hours of the morning. Too wired for sleep, he emptied six cans of beer down his throat, and dug down under the floorboards to bring up several videos to keep him entertained until he could fall asleep in the chair. Now that Frances would be staying at the hospital for a whole week, he would not even have to hide them away.

***

Once the baby had been home for a few months, Martin discovered that the novelty of being a new father had started to wear off quite considerably. Colin refused to sleep for longer than an hour at a time, and he felt desperately tired, on edge, and permanently sexually frustrated. Frances' body, temporarily damaged by childbirth, was mostly off limits, and he felt cast out and redundant as his wife cooed and fussed over their son. After a first attempt at restoring their interrupted sex life six weeks after the birth, he found himself wishing the doctor had put in an extra stitch or two when he had repaired her episiotomy.

Late at night when he brought the videos out from under the floorboards, they somehow failed to satisfy him as much as they had initially done. He began to search further afield for his entertainment, hating himself for seeking out a prostitute for the first time when working away overnight in London, but telling himself that it was just sex, so it did not matter. The woman's face was instantly forgettable, but what he did remember about that night was that she was agreeable to everything that Frances had previously refused to do, and with the light on as an added bonus. The forty pounds she charged was well worth the money, and he made sure to pay in cash so that there was no record on their bank statement.

He began to look forward to business trips away. The one night stands came and went, and he was sure that Frances felt more relieved now that he no longer needed to pester her for sex as much. He loved her just as much as ever, but she was too wrapped up in her new-found motherhood, and try as he might, the missionary position in total darkness was definitely not doing it for him anymore.

CHAPTER 7

He watched her face intently as she opened up his carefully wrapped present, and felt a small stab of disappointment when the contents failed to elicit the response he had anticipated.

"This really isn't me, Martin."

He forced a smile at the sight of his wife's distasteful look as she held up a pair of see-through black crotchless panties between the tips of her forefingers and thumbs.

"Sorry. I thought you might be willing to spice up our love life a little bit. You'd look gorgeous in them."

"What's wrong with our love life?"

He wanted to tell her that he was bored out of his mind with it, but decided to keep the sad fact to himself.

"Nothing! Nothing at all!" He lied effortlessly. "Forget it."

As he busied himself taking the panties from her and collecting up the wrapping paper, he was aware of her eyes boring into the side of his face.

"Are you still watching porn?"

His heart skipped a beat as he turned to face her.

"No, of course not! Why do you ask?"

"Because I expect the girls in the videos you watch are wearing that sort of thing, aren't they?"

Her gaze flicked down to rest upon the unwelcome present in his hands. Martin shrugged his shoulders and let the lie slip out convincingly.

"I don't remember, and I'm not watching porn videos anymore."

"Is that so?"

He could tell by the expression on her face that she remained unconvinced.

***

Colin grew to be a lively toddler, into everything and anything. He was aware that Frances, an only child herself, did not want their boy to be without a brother or sister. Having been brought up with four siblings himself, he remembered the noise, the arguments, and the total lack of privacy. He wanted the best for his son, and gave a last-ditch plea.

"Why not just stick with just one child?"

He could see her shaking her head before he'd even finished speaking.

"I grew up lonely. I don't want that for Colin. Besides, think of all the sex we can have while we're practising to become parents again!"

Sex in the dark with Frances needed some degree of augmentation, and with Janet he had not only re-wired her triple garage, but had also found just the right person to bridge the sexual chasm between himself and Frances. Rich and bored at home with no meaningful purpose in life, his latest mistress was a little older, but eager and willing to carry out every single one of his mind-bending fantasies. Giving a new membership at the gym as an excuse for his absence whenever Janet's husband Matt was away, he was encouraged to take quick advantage of his mistress's eagerness to experiment with new sexual positions, and BDSM in particular. Her cinema room held an impressive collection of pornographic videos, and by the time six months had passed he had watched all of them, reaching new heights of pleasure with Janet, and managing to impregnate Frances for a second time in the dark whilst calling up images of Janet in chains and black lace to help him out at the crucial moment.

***

Martin quashed the urge to drink another pint of beer, and realised that his wife had been right after all. His habit had long ago ended whatever semblance of a sex life they'd had. He'd been satisfied with their lovemaking in the early days of their marriage, but the excitement of porn had triumphed over Frances' ministrations in the dark. For years he had been unable to make love to his wife without thinking about the latest video he had watched, or even reminding himself of Janet as she was then, spread-eagled enticingly upon her black silken sheets.

He stood up and made his way past increasingly vociferous drinkers to the pub's exit, hating himself for having always shouted down Frances' fears in his ignorance of the effects on his marriage of watching other people have sex. His wife had a good head on her shoulders. She had told it to him straight many times that he was addicted, but he knew he wasn't. He had treated her quiet explanations with derision; minimising the consequences of his actions and determined to resist being told what to, especially by a woman.

He did not want to go home and face her, but he knew he must.

***

She was sitting quietly reading when he came into the front room. She looked up at him briefly before returning to her book, and his heart melted. He loved her more than words could say.

"Hi."

She ignored his greeting and kept her eyes downcast as she spoke. "Where did you get to?"

"I went into The Milestone for a pint."

"That figures." She sighed and shook her head slightly.

"Just the one though."

"Yeah, sure."

He knew he was stuffed. Try as he might to redeem himself, his wife would not or could not believe a single word that came out of his mouth.

***

"So, Martin…" Rhona folded her arms and looked at him. "Do you feel more ready to talk today, or would you like Frances to take a turn?"

Martin shrugged.

"All I want to say is that I've given up porn, and only drink the odd pint now and then. The trouble is that Frances doesn't believe me."

Rhona nodded sagely.

"This can happen when a learned behaviour has gone on for a long time. Trust has to be earned again, to re-build the marriage."

"How can I do that?" Martin gave a huge sigh.

"Talk to your wife in those three communication sessions every week that I mentioned before. She will let you know what she wants you to do."

"Sure." Martin looked sideways at Frances, who remained impassive. "Whatever it takes."

"But we've gone over this time and time again." Frances kept her gaze on Rhona. "It's no good. He always goes back to porn and drinking, and is probably still having sex with prostitutes when he goes away. He can't help it, the behaviour's too ingrained in him."

"You see the problem I have?" Martin's voice rose a semitone. "It's hopeless!"

Rhona took a sip of water.

"Frances, do you think that at some point you will be able to trust Martin again and forgive him?"

"I don't know. He hasn't given me any reason to in the past." Frances sighed.

"Well, a *don't know* is better than a no." Martin's voice sounded momentarily upbeat. "At least that's better than what you've been saying before. And anyway, what about *you* recording *me*? Have you stopped doing that?"

"Of course I have."

"So I have to learn to trust *you* as well, don't I?"

He noticed how his wife remained silent and appeared somewhat uncomfortable at his statement.

"Would either of you care to elaborate a little bit?" Rhona looked up inquisitively.

He heard Frances give a little cough of embarrassment before speaking.

"Oh…I wanted to get my own back I suppose. Do unto those who do unto you and all that."

"And you did?" Rhona asked with more than a degree of interest.

"Yeah… I suppose so. I brought a recording device home from work and hid it in Martin's office. It told me all I wanted to know. Surprise, surprise, he didn't like it when he found out, but as far as I was concerned, he'd had a little taste of his own medicine."

"Where is it now?" He looked down at her bag.

"Who knows? Back where it came from I expect." Frances followed his gaze. "This was all years ago. It's certainly not in my bag."

"So you're not recording everything that's being said here?"

"Of course not." Frances shook her head. "You'll just have to believe me."

CHAPTER 8

FRANCES

There was a conference on and therefore no clinics to type for a week. Frances came to the swift conclusion that nobody would miss the office's new mini-disc recorder if she took it home for a short while. She lifted the machine out of the filing cabinet and put it in her bag whilst her colleagues were at lunch. For weeks she had wracked her brain to try and think of a way to catch him out, and then the answer came to her in a flash, as she carried out some much needed filing. *Of course!* If she hid the recorder in Martin's office, she might be able to find out if he was still logging in to porn sites or taking part in phone sex. With two sexually-curious and computer literate teenage boys in the house, she had to make sure that neither Colin nor Richard came across their father's stash of computer porn by accident if they logged in to do their homework.

She could hardly wait to return home, turn the key in the lock, and seek out a good place to hide the recorder before the boys and Martin came back. Typing clinic letters part time did not earn her a great deal of money, but it did give her a couple of hours to herself at the end of every weekday afternoon. She grinned ruefully to herself that it had also given her a delightful chance for a kind of schoolgirl crush on Graham, but that was definitely another story.

The house was still and silent as she locked the front door behind her and took off her outdoor shoes. She loosened her grip on the handles of her bag after taking the mini-disc player out of the front zipped pocket. As her bag fell to the floor, she almost ran up the stairs towards the study. The computer's now blank screen that had displayed a multitude of Martin's secrets stared back at her defiantly, offering up a challenge.

Frances' gaze rested upon a mobile air-conditioning machine in one corner near the window. There was a small space between the bottom of the machine and the floor, large enough however for her hand to slip underneath and deposit the machine. They were not in the height of summer, and so she knew the air-con unit would remain where it was. It would be perfect for the coming autumnal Friday mornings, when Martin stayed at home to phone potential customers and to sort out his invoices. Her heart beat a little faster at the thought that in only two days' time she would know whether her husband was telling her the truth or not. *Had he stopped looking at porn?* She would love to be able to believe him but her female intuition or gut instinct, call it what you will, was telling her something different.

***

She could hear water splashing in their en-suite shower room. Frances felt in her pocket for the recorder, took her chance and dashed into the office, switching it on and slipping it quickly under the air-con unit. As she came out of the office, she heard his voice calling out.

"Fran! Where's the new toothpaste?"

She kept her voice even as she walked into the bedroom and stood in front of him.

"In the cupboard under the sink." She pointed to confirm her answer. "I'll wait to see the boys off on the school bus, and then I'll go to the hospital. Have fun with the invoices."

"Yeah."

She gave him a peck on the cheek and then went downstairs to chivvy their sons along with breakfast, willing the day away. Even though Graham was away in the Caribbean with his family and had no idea of her feelings, she was missing the sight of him along the hospital corridors. She was also impatient to discover any evidence from the recorder, and had no idea how on earth she was going to concentrate on typing up two dermatology clinics.

***

She could hear him talking on the phone when she ambled upstairs at 3.30 as nonchalantly as she could, inwardly worried about how much longer the batteries on the recorder would work. To arouse his suspicion with low battery bleeps emanating from under the air-con unit was a horror she did not really want to think about. She had to find some way to get him out of the office. She waited until he had replaced the receiver, and then stood idly in front of him in the doorway.

"Martin, could you check my front tyres please? The steering felt a bit funny driving home today."

"Sure." He turned towards her. "Now or later?"

"Oh, now if you don't mind? It's youth club tonight, and I'm babysitting for Mary for a couple of hours as well."

She hoped he did not need to phone his sister during the evening.

"Okay." He stood up. "Can you get the phone if it rings? I'm waiting for a call."

"Yeah; I'll wait here until you come back."

Acting quickly as the front door clicked shut, Frances grabbed the mini-disc player and glanced at it briefly. Its recording time had ended several hours ago, and the battery display was showing only three bars.

With some relief she switched the machine off and dropped it into her coat pocket, sinking down into the battered leather chair and hearing its familiar squeak as she shifted about nervously. She looked at the computer screen showing the previous month-end figures and wondered whether she had time to check his viewing history, but changed her mind as she heard the front door open again.

"No, they're fine." Martin ran up the stairs. "I checked them with the pressure gauge. Has the phone rang?"

"No." She shook her head and stood up. "I'll leave you to it then. I've got a casserole to prepare."

"Sounds good. Stick some dumplings in; I don't care if they clog me up."

***

"Mum, I don't want to go to youth club anymore."

Richard yawned and eyed the church hall frontage with a degree of ennui.

"Well, just for tonight then, seeing as we're already here." Frances felt desperate for an hour on her own to listen to the recorder in peace in the car. "Colin seems to like it."

"Only because Keira goes."

"What a load of sh….rubbish you talk." Colin's adolescent vocal cords croaked in an alarmingly quick response from the back seat. "And it's my turn to sit in the front on the way back."

"Drop dead."

"Out you get, boys." Frances sighed. "Dad will come back at ten for you."

She waved to Richard, looking miserably over his shoulder at her as the car's engine burst into life. Her sensitive and artistic son was growing up with an entirely different personality to that of his brother. Her two boys were like chalk and cheese.

CHAPTER 9

"So, Frances…" Rhona smiled and opened up her notebook. "Where did we get to last time?"

"Martin was asking whether I'd stopped recording him."

"Ah yes." Rhona nodded. "And have you?"

"I said I had last time, but actually I haven't." Frances sighed. "I can't stop. The whole porn detective thing has become *my* addiction. We're just going round and round in circles, playing mind games with each other. When I was made redundant at the hospital I bought myself one of those up to the minute digital voice recorders so that I could carry on with what I'd started."

Beside her on the sofa she heard Martin take in a quick breath, and saw his hands briefly ball into fists. She ran her fingers through her hair distractedly, and decided to keep her eyes fixed firmly on Rhona.

"So the problem is continuing, that neither of you trust the other one?" Rhona looked intently at Frances.

"Yes, that's right. He's still looking at porn. I can hear the gasping and groaning going on, even though he's obviously wearing headphones. He must have the volume up extremely loud for it to be picked up by the recorder. So he's still lying to me after all this time, which makes me want to carry on recording him to find out if he's telling the truth, but so far he isn't. I'm sick of living like this."

Frances had finished speaking, and Rhona jotted down a few notes before replying.

"Eventually, would you like to patch things up with your husband and get back to where you used to be?"

Frances shrugged.

"It's Martin's wish for us to be happy, but I don't know if it's possible now. The trust is gone. How can you live happily with somebody that you don't trust and who lies to you all the time?"

She felt Martin's eyes on her, but could not look at him as he spoke.

"I've not long stopped, but I can assure you that I don't watch porn anymore. I've given it up. You must have a recording that's a few weeks old."

She felt tears spring to her eyes. Her husband was the biggest mindfuck on the planet.

"It's not easy, but the answer is to ultimately agree to forgive, and to give each other another chance." Rhona addressed both of them. "Trust will need to be built up again. You will need to show each other by deeds and not words that you can both be trusted."

***

The seat gave the familiar squeak as Martin sat down. Frances, alone in the car as darkness fell, closed her eyes and listened, trying to ignore the background hiss of the recorder's volume set high to overcome traffic passing down the little country lane.

After the squeak came a sigh and a yawn, and Frances was surprised to hear light snoring about five minutes later. The fact that Martin might have gone back to sleep after she and the boys had gone out had never occurred to her. When their landline phone jangled she nearly jumped out of her skin, and laughed briefly as her husband seemed to suffer the same fate.

"Yeah?"

He coughed to clear his throat. The chair squeaked as he sat up, and Frances wondered about the identity of the person on the other end of the line.

"Yeah, I left a message. I can start next week."

A customer. Frances felt pleased that Martin's business was going from strength to strength. Word was getting about that he was efficient, good at his job, and didn't charge too high a price. It had taken courage to branch out on his own when the boys were babies, but currently it seemed that his efforts had finally paid off.

After the phone call came what sounded like a can's ring pull. Frances was dismayed at the thought of her husband drinking alcohol so early in the mornings. The loud burping that followed was evidence of the fact, and she shook her head sorrowfully in the darkness. *If his drinking was getting out of hand, then the profit he was making from his regular clutch of customers would soon start to be eroded.*

She checked her watch. Martin wouldn't be expecting her for another hour at least. She started to wind through the silences. A low moan made her prick up her ears and her heart began to beat a little faster, feeling some relief at not recognising her own voice. However, the noise of sex was definitely unmistakeable, coupled with the odd word spoken in an American accent; a man's urgent tones as he reached a climax, and a woman gasping and groaning for all she was worth.

The proof she needed was in her hands. Frances, dismayed beyond belief, switched off the mini-disc player, but then had second thoughts and brought it back to life. She also needed to know whether Martin was having another affair or still seeing Triple Garage Janet.

The rest of the tape was uneventful apart from half an hour of porn and the office chair squeaking and creaking as Martin became more and more excited. After he had relieved himself she turned it off for good. All she wanted to do now was to go home and get in the shower; she felt dirty.

***

Nobody at work had noticed the mini-disc's absence. Frances, still uncertain as to whether Martin was seeing anybody else, made sure she had deleted any tell-tale evidence before slipping it back into the filing cabinet, vowing to take it home again soon in the foreseeable future. She was pleased with her find. The mini-disc would be a valuable ally in the days to come.

CHAPTER 10

MARTIN

He tried to stop the irritation he felt from showing in his voice. Keeping his expression impassive, he ignored Frances and focused on Rhona.

"So you see, it's hopeless. She must have been recording me for years without me knowing, before she told me how she was doing it. I have no idea if she's now got a recorder in every room in the house. I'm frightened even to make an innocent phone call to a customer in case Frances misconstrues the conversation and thinks I'm having an affair. Every time I go out of the front door I imagine her checking through the viewing history on my computer. I've had all the stuff off the shelves in my office several times, trying to find listening devices. Pathetic as it may seem, I'm even wary about farting out loud anymore."

The *tut* of annoyance emanating from his right was loud enough not to pass him by.

"At least your genitals weren't on screen for all and sundry to see without your permission."

Martin sighed with the sure and certain knowledge that although his wife did not have the first idea about setting up a secret camera, figuratively speaking she did have him squarely and securely by the short and curlies. He crossed his legs in an imagined effort to guard against further emasculation, and tried to concentrate on Rhona's voice.

"What I'm going to suggest is that you take a holiday together. Leave your mobile phones, iPads and whatever at home, so there is just the two of you. Take time out to talk and enjoy each other's company like you used to do. What do you say?"

"Fine by me." Martin nodded. "What about you, Fran?"

He was aware that his wife appeared less than enamoured with the idea while ignoring his question completely and speaking directly to the counsellor.

"Our daughter-in-law is due to have her second child in a few weeks. I need to be on hand to help out with Charlie, the eldest."

Martin heard a clock ticking somewhere in the silence of the room before Rhona answered.

"Can her mother not do this?"

Frances shook her head.

"It's a bit difficult, seeing as how she passed away two years ago."

"Oh."

The counsellor's bonhomie was falling away fast as it met the brick wall of his wife's non-compliance. Martin likened the whole scenario to flogging a dead horse.

"We can do it after the baby's born. Shall I book something Fran?"

He turned to see his wife shrugging her shoulders.

"Whatever."

Rhona's smile became fixed, and he caught the quick glance at her watch.

"The holiday will be a good way forward for both of you. Book somewhere nice and sunny, and get to know each other again. Come back and see me afterwards and let me know how you get on. But Martin, do try and give Frances proof that you're not watching porn. Don't delete your phone or computer history; let her find out for herself that you're now telling the truth. By wiping everything clean, you're only making matters worse."

He knew it was the right thing to do. Martin nodded in agreement.

"Will do. I'll leave my phone downstairs at night too; then Fran will know it's not in my room."

"Excellent!" Rhona gave Martin a thumbs-up.

***

All he wanted to do was turn back the clock. Back to when his wife looked at him like their daughter-in-law looked at their son. Too many times Fran had told him to give up the porn, and like a fool he had stubbornly resisted, hating to be told what to do as though he were a child of five. Her pleas had fallen on deaf ears, indeed her ultimatums had just made him more secretive. He remembered how he'd gloated in triumph when he'd thought of using headphones; grinning at the stupid games his wife was playing in order to catch him out. *There was always an easy way to get one over on her.* However, he now wished he'd taken her innate intelligence into consideration.

Martin selected first gear and pulled away from the kerb, taking a quick glance at Frances, whose face was devoid of any emotion.

"Shall we stop by at the travel agent's on the way home?"

"If you like." She shrugged. "But I don't see how going on holiday is going to help to change my mind. I still want a break from you."

"No you don't." He tried to keep the desperation out of his voice. "You're just pissed off. You'll feel differently after a week or two in the sun."

"Is that so?"

He was aware that Frances had turned her head away from him to look out of the window. He tried to stem a rising panic that this time he had actually gone too far; never before had she seemed so antagonistic.

"I'm so sorry, love, for being such a bastard. I'll make it up to you, I promise."

Her reply cut through the icy atmosphere in the car like a knife.

"You can't help it. You were born that way."

***

He turned off the engine and looked through the travel agent's window. For once he could see no queues forming inside. Ignoring the fact that he had parked on double yellow lines, he turned to give Frances his best impression of a hearty smile.

"Are you sure you don't want to come in?"

"No thanks; just book whatever you want, but make it for about three or four months' time."

He hid a stab of disappointment.

"I'll see if they have any last minute cruise places if you like?"

He waited in vain for her expression to lighten at the thought of two weeks in the sun in the middle of winter. Her reply sent an autumn chill through his bones despite the early October sunshine.

"If they have, pay extra and book two cabins."

***

He could see her in his peripheral vision, sitting grimly in the passenger seat and staring straight ahead. The thought of paying double for two cabins when every other cosy couple on the ship would be sharing had not been what he'd had in mind. However, ignoring the travel agent's look of surprise he plumped for two inside cabins next door to each other, paid a hefty deposit, grabbed some paperwork and a brochure, and walked back out to the car.

"We're going on the Mardi Gras Celebration cruise in February. The girl said there's some excellent excursions too." He waved the brochure in the air as he climbed back into the driver's seat. "Want to have a look? We'll be able to swim with dolphins as well."

"Later."

He was encouraged as she sifted through the brochure on the journey home.

"And there'll be one of those old cotton plantations to look around."

He saw her shrug out of the corner of his eye. When she spoke, her voice was flat and without emotion.

"You won't like that; you never want to look around National Trust places in your own backyard, let alone somewhere four and a half thousand miles away."

He stifled a bitter retort and pressed a little harder on the accelerator.

"Give us a break; I'm really trying to make you happy."

Her reply was an audible sigh, resonating around the silent interior of the car.

CHAPTER 11

She delved down behind the cupboard on the upstairs landing. By the time he had flushed the toilet she was back in her own bedroom with her spoils; another scratchy playback on high volume for listening into the early hours. The previous two had failed to produce the evidence she'd hoped for, and she was sick of the whole thing. It felt to her sometimes as though she was going stark, staring mad.

Somebody else was driving their limousine into Janet's triple garage; she'd found out that much by listening in on the last recording. Just who he *was* seeing now remained a mystery. Of course, she realised that now he knew what she was up to, he would probably wait until he was out on the road and make calls on his mobile in private, but she had the answer to that; she would bug his van instead.

She thanked her lucky stars that he had agreed to separate bedrooms now that the boys had left home and were off their hands. Feigning a headache and retiring early, she donned a pair of headphones and switched on the digital voice recorder, laying wide awake in the darkness with her brain on high alert for any tell-tale moaning or gasping. There was nothing to be heard. Unable to sleep, she fumed silently at Martin's innate ability to always circumvent her carefully laid plans. It seemed as though he was always one step ahead of her.

Frances tossed and turned until she was boiling hot under the sheets, which became all twisted up around her middle. Giving up on sleep for the rest of the night she climbed out of bed and padded downstairs to make a cup of tea, biting her lip in anger when she heard loud snoring emanating from Martin's bedroom.

His phone sat on the kitchen table where he had promised to leave it. She picked it up and entered the passcode he had told her as she switched on the kettle. She could see his viewing history was unremarkable. However, she did not trust him one iota, and she sighed at the thought of now having to work out his new method of accessing porn.

The kettle switched itself off. Frances poured some water onto a teabag, and then opened the fridge door, blinking at the sudden light. She carried the remains of a pint of milk over to the kitchen table and poured its contents into a mug of tea, sighing again heavily and hating the fact that she was so reliant on a man to put food on the table. As she sipped the welcome brew in the small hours of her 56th year on the earth, she made a conscious decision to be more assertive and find herself another job. After the redundancy and ensuing dreary days of being a housewife, Frances was filled with a kind of dread at the thought of going out and competing with the young and sassy in the cut-throat world of job-hunting, but she knew what she had to do in order to be true to herself and live a porn-free life. She was unaware of time passing as she contemplated her future. The immediate weeks would be filled with looking after Charlie, but after that the world was hers for the taking. She swallowed another mouthful of tea and wondered if the world could actually *be* taken by a middle-aged woman only used to typing letters and doing bookwork, hoovering, dusting, looking after children, and cooking dinners.

***

Looking after children had always come naturally to her. Little Charlie at two years old was an absolute delight. When the call to arms came in the middle of the night from a nervous-sounding Colin, Frances found herself firing on all cylinders. She had already prepared Charlie's travel cot in her room, and she could hardly wait to cuddle her grandson's warm little body. Not even bothering to wake Martin, she was dressed in minutes, and out of the door. The car started at once, and as she eased it into first gear and pulled away she looked forward to the reality of a new grandchild within a few hours. Charlie's birth had been quick, and the second was all set to arrive even quicker.

Just how quick the birth would be was quite obvious by the time she arrived at the house. One look at her daughter-in-law pushing for all her might caused a temporary abandonment of all her worries and cares. She tried to keep a calm demeanour as her son sweated by the bed-head whilst little Charlie slept on in the room next door in blissful ignorance. She took in the scene of Colin with one arm around Jane's back, who was propped forward and grunting in a kind of animalistic fashion.

"I've called an ambulance, Mum!" Colin took his wife's hand. "It's all happened so fast – there was no time to drive her to hospital!"

"Not to worry." Frances swallowed hard. "I'll go and get some towels to put under that duvet. It looks as though we might have to deliver the baby ourselves."

Colin nodded.

"Leave the front door open for the ambulance people."

Frances ran downstairs, yanked open the front door, and then ran back up to the airing cupboard and grabbed as many towels as she could see. Wide awake despite the early hour, she flew into the bedroom and deposited them around a straining Jane.

"You're doing fine." Frances hoped her voice sounded more confident than she felt. "The ambulance is on its way."

"So sorry!" Jane sobbed and clutched her abdomen. "I never thought it would happen so quickly!"

Frances kept her voice bright.

"No worries! That baby is going to be here before Charlie wakes up."

Another contraction hit. Jane retched with pain, and Frances saw the head beginning to crown. Just in time she remembered the midwife's advice during her own two labours.

"Try not to push; just let the head come out on its own. Colin, can you get a bowl or something?"

In the background she heard the comforting sound of an ambulance siren. Her son leapt up like a startled fawn and sped off in the direction of the kitchen, returning panting and carrying a washing up bowl. Jane retched again into the bowl and gave a small push. With a great deal of relief and a welling up of tears, Frances saw her grandbaby's head appear as the paramedics ran breathless into the room.

"She's doing fine."

She suddenly wanted to sob as one of the paramedics eased out the shoulders. One final push and her grandson slid from his warm, safe environment onto a towel, letting all occupants in the room know in no uncertain terms how furious he felt at his sudden expulsion into the cold, unforgiving world. Sighing, she blinked back her tears and felt privileged to have witnessed such a happy occasion. Frances smiled as Colin cuddled his wife.

"It's a boy, Jane! We've got another son!"

Jane fell back limply onto the pillow as the paramedic wrapped up the baby and presented him to his mother, who immediately and expertly put him to the breast. Silence pervaded the room, broken only by the sound of contented sucking. She squeezed Colin's hand just as one of the paramedics produced a large kidney bowl.

"I'm going to give you a small injection to help deliver the afterbirth."

Jane nodded and Frances departed downstairs on shaky legs to produce a tray of tea and biscuits and give the two parents some degree of privacy. After Jane and the baby were eventually carried downstairs to the waiting ambulance, Frances helped Colin clear up as best she could. By the time she fell asleep on the settee it was 04:45. She had never felt so exhausted in her whole life, but she felt privileged to have witnessed the birth of little Frankie John Andrews.

CHAPTER 12

"You could be just what we're looking for Mrs Andrews."

Frances nearly fell off her chair in surprise. Deana Smith was nodding and smiling as though she really meant it.

"Really?"

"Of course! You've spent your life caring for your family, and we mustn't let all that experience go to waste. Our carers do undertake part time Health and Social Care courses at the college, and you would be encouraged to study for a diploma. New carers also have to undergo a check for any criminal records."

"Wow!" Frances could not suppress a grin. "Me going to college at the age of fifty five?"

"It would be evening classes in your own time, because obviously you would be working here during the day. However, we do pay for the course." Deana nodded. "Would you be willing to undergo a three month probation period?"

"Absolutely!" Frances could not believe her luck. "When can I start?"

"Well, what about the first of December? That gives you a fortnight or so to get used to the idea, and for us to do the CRB check. College would begin next September; it's not worth starting until then, as you'd do better at the beginning of a new course rather than trying to catch up a quarter of the way through."

Frances silently agreed.

"And I would have gained some knowledge by working here by then."

"Oh yes, you'd have learned quite a lot by September." Deana jotted down a few notes. "I'll get all the paperwork ready for you to fill in. Leave it a week or so, and then come in and sign on the dotted line, so to speak."

"We've got a holiday booked in February, by the way." Frances' mood suddenly darkened at the thought of it. "February the nineteenth until March the fourth."

"Oh?" Deana looked up with interest. "Where to?"

"A cruise that takes in the Mardi Gras in New Orleans, as well as Grand Cayman and Cozumel." Frances decided not to show her displeasure at the thought of having to spend a fortnight with Martin. "And we'll be swimming with the dolphins in Costa Maya."

"How wonderful!" Deana clapped her hands momentarily. "I'll make a note of those dates. Thanks for letting me know. And now, would you like to see around the home?"

"Yes please." Frances nodded. "I'd like that very much.

***

The television was blaring away, but she could tell that the group of elderly ladies sitting in a circle around it were not really following the programme. Some were asleep, some fiddled with their clothing, and one raised her arm immediately on seeing a member of staff.

"I want a wee."

Frances watched as Deana walked up to the old lady and took her hand.

"Mavis took you to the toilet half an hour ago Mrs. Jones."

Frances felt helpless as the old woman's eyes met hers.

"I want a wee."

"Shall I help her to the toilet?" Frances glanced at Deana. "I don't mind."

Deana shook her head.

"She'll have you running there and back every five minutes."

Frances felt somewhat disappointed at the manager's remark, but decided not to reply. As they left the sitting room and made their way upstairs, she could still hear Mrs Jones' desperate voice pleading for help. She made a mental note for the future to ignore the manager's advice.

Along the first floor landing Frances found a few rooms occupied by bed-bound or chair-bound elderly residents who needed all care. Deana kept her voice low as they stood in the doorways:

"You'll learn the best way of turning them and how to use the hoist to protect your back. Never think that you can lift them on your own; I want my carers to be fit and healthy, and not having to take time off to visit chiropractors or osteopaths. You'll be shadowing one of the senior carers until you've learned the ropes."

Frances met the rheumy eyes of a somewhat rotund elderly gentleman, and silently wondered why Deana had voiced the assumption that she might have even considered lifting somebody nearly twice her body weight. She nodded in reply.

"I look forward to it."

***

She walked into the front room and noticed with distaste how her husband was sprawled out on the sofa flicking through TV channels at four thirty in the afternoon. He looked up at her with a flicker of interest.

"Where have you been? Out with *him*?"

She wondered how much longer she could string out the imaginary affair with Graham, but nonetheless felt proud of herself and could not hide a self-satisfied smile.

"I've found myself a job."

She saw at once the effect of her words, and watched him intently as he turned off the remote control and sat up straighter.

"Doing what?"

"I'll be working part-time shifts at the Sunset Care Home just off the High Street. It's time I started earning my own money. The boys have gone; I want to do something other than hoover the house and cook your dinner."

For a brief moment she saw an expression of utter defeat cross his features.

"What about my bookwork? Will you still do the invoices and stuff?"

"I can do that in-between times. I need to get out of this house, Martin."

He shrugged.

"You know you don't *have* to go to work. We've got enough money."

She sighed and looked at him in exasperation.

"You just don't get it, do you? The reason I've been looking for a job is to get away from *you*! You were right, the council wouldn't give me a flat, I've got no income, and we can't afford to run two homes. I'm bloody well stuck here, therefore it's best if I make myself scarce most of the time."

She watched him run a hand distractedly through his hair, signalling as she well knew, his lack of control over a situation.

"Or is all this a ploy just to give you more time to see *him*?"

"Oh, don't keep going on about that." She sat down dejectedly beside him. "It was never going anywhere. He's got three kids."

"So who is he then?"

"I told you; a doctor at the hospital. We both reached for the same packet of bog roll in Sainsbury's at the same time."

"Yeah, he definitely sounds shitty to me."

Frances stood up.

"Look; I've told you where I'll be, and it's up to you to believe me. I did wonder if it might work with the doctor, but I was just kidding myself. Perhaps you should look at your own track record with other women before you start criticising *me*."

As she turned on her heel to walk out of the room, she heard him spring up from the sofa. A hand pulled on her shoulder, spinning her back around to face him again.

"I want to know who he is!"

She felt intimidated by his obvious physical strength and power, but inwardly satisfied that she had rattled his cage.

"He's somebody I was attracted to, and strangely enough he was attracted to me as well. But it's all over with. I've left the hospital, so just let's leave it at that."

His body sagged as though she had punched the air from his lungs.

"Will you ever tell me who it is?"

She shook her head.

"No."

CHAPTER 13

He glanced idly at the post-it note stuck onto the side of the cereal box:

'My first shift starts at 07:30, so I left while you were in the shower. Back later.'

He sighed ruefully and remembered a time when her notes would be overflowing with kisses not only underneath the text, but trailing in a loving line all the way around the edges of the page. He pulled the note off its resting place with more force than was necessary, poured out some cornflakes and ate mechanically, viewing the vacant seat opposite with a stab of disappointment. After eating he washed up his plate and cup and wiped down the surfaces methodically, knowing that she liked a clean kitchen.

Who the fuck was that fucking doctor fucking his wife? He picked up a clean pair of overalls sitting on top of the washing machine and walked out into the hall, grabbing his car keys from a hook by the front door. The sun had not even begun to rise, and the windscreen of his van was covered in a thick sheet of ice. Martin opened the driver's door and rooted around in the back for his scraper, giving up after a fruitless five minute search. He turned on the engine, ramped up the heat to its highest level, and waited morosely for the de-mister to do its work.

The radio presenter was too over-jolly for such an early morning show. Martin rubbed the inside of the windscreen with the sleeve of his jacket, yawned loudly, and let out a belch that reverberated around the inside of the van. When he could see enough of the road he pulled away from the kerb, letting a curse slip from his lips at the thought of spending the rest of his day house bashing on a freezing cold building site.

"Fuck!"

He purposely took the route that went past the old people's home. For a brief moment he considered popping in to surprise her, but then thought better of it. He accelerated harder and turned the radio up.

*****

It had been a long, freezing day, and he was thoroughly pissed off. As he walked back to the van at six o'clock carrying his toolbox under one arm he could see a sheen of ice covering the van's windscreen again. Wrenching open the back of the van and determined to find his scraper, he threw his toolbox inside, switched on a torch, and moved a reel of cable to one side. As he lifted up a tarpaulin to investigate further, he spotted a small rectangular device tucked in underneath one of the tarpaulin's folds. Picking it up out of curiosity, he moved closer to a street lamp to get a better view. By the lamp's orange glow he could see a red light in one corner of the display screen, which also showed a digital clock face that had been ticking away for over eleven hours. Just below the screen he read '*Digital Voice Recorder VN-8500PC*'.

He had found it! His day had suddenly taken a turn for the better. Martin felt like doing a little dance there and then down the street in his dusty overalls.

"Yessss!"

He carefully moved the recorder around to his lower back and emitted a long stream of flatulence. Then, grinning, he took a claw hammer out of his toolbox, put the voice recorder on the ground, and with a great deal of satisfaction stamped on it with his hobnailed boot. Just to ensure its demise, he then gave it a couple of whacks with the hammer before kicking it across the street, twisting his features into a maniacal grin in the process.

***

She was asleep on the settee as he walked into the darkness of the front room and switched on the lamp. He watched her as, flustered, she jumped up quickly in the manner of a startled fawn.

"I was knackered. I fell asleep."

"Heavy first day? Shall I get fish and chips for dinner then?"

"Good idea." She nodded and then sat down again, rubbing her eyes. "I'll get used to it."

He shrugged.

"I've already told you; you don't have to go out to work."

"Let's not start that again. Shall I come with you in the van?"

"If you like, although you won't find anything when I go into the shop."

He caught a glimpse of feigned puzzlement on her features.

"What do you mean?"

"I *mean* that your voice recorder is now playing back my farts into the great hereafter." He turned and walked into the hallway with as much dignity as he could muster. "Cod or haddock?"

"Neither." She slumped back against the back of the settee. "I'm suddenly not hungry anymore."

"Suit yourself."

He thought he heard a faint scream of despair as he slammed the door behind him.

***

He could smell an appetising aroma of toast as he sat down at the kitchen table carrying a warm parcel wrapped in white paper. She appeared in his peripheral vision and watched him unwrapping his meal and spearing a flaky piece of fish with his fork.

"Fancy a chip?"

"Look, I'm sorry, okay?" She picked a chip out of the paper. "Does that make us even?"

He wolfed down a large piece of batter and shook his head.

"No, because I got rid of the camera ages ago, so it's *advantage Frances*, as they say."

"If it makes you feel any better, I haven't heard anything recently."

He rolled his eyes briefly heavenwards.

"That's because I've stopped looking at porn; I've *told* you that already. "He waggled his fork in her direction. "You're wasting your time."

He heard a sigh escape from her lips as she sat down beside him.

"But I have to find that out for myself."

He stuffed three chips into his mouth, and then sat back and looked at her as he chewed.

"So what's next? Is my bedroom bugged? Is there something nasty in the shed?"

"Yeah, your porn mags probably." She took another chip. "I haven't got another recorder, so don't worry."

"But I do worry." He gave her a steely look. "I'm getting very concerned about you; you're taking all this to extremes."

"So… prove to me that you've stopped."

"I can't." He shrugged. "You'll have to take my word for it."

"And therein lies the eternal problem."

He sprinkled some vinegar to enhance the fish's flavour.

"And how do I know you've finished with the doctor?"

"Well, that's easy." She gave him a thin smile. "You can take my word for it."

He screwed up the paper into a tight ball and threw it with force across the room. *Their mind games were doing his fucking head in!*

CHAPTER 14

FRANCES

She looked on as Sylvia Dalton's practised fingers closed the old woman's eyes. Rose Benwell, complaining to the last, had finally been granted her wish. Frances mused that the only time she had been this close to death was when she had sat with her mother's coffin in the Chapel of Rest.

She found it quite disturbing to hear Sylvia humming quietly to herself as she plugged the introituses, and instead imagined Rose already haranguing a steadfast St. Peter standing stoically at the entrance to the pearly gates with his arms folded and head shaking from side to side.

"Need any help?"

Frances came out of her reverie and turned towards the sound of the voice. Mavis Burtenshaw, a soiled incontinence pad in one hand, stood in the doorway.

"Nearly done now." Sylvia grinned and pointed a finger in the direction of the pad. "Couldn't you wait?"

Mavis rolled her eyes.

"Albert's peeing all over the place. He took the bunch of dahlias out of his vase and used that. I found the pad on top of his head."

"He probably thought it was his cap." Sylvia shrugged. "I had to put it in the washing machine this morning; he'd filled it up."

"What a bloody job!" Mavis sighed. "Why you want to work here Frances, I don't know. I'll put the kettle on; thank God it's tea break time.

Frances smiled at Mavis and watched Sylvia wrapping Rose in a sheet and tagging the big toe of her right foot.

"You can do the next one, and *I'll* watch. It won't be long before you get your chance."

"Oh goody." Frances could not help but smile. "I can't wait."

"Deana will sort the rest out with the undertakers, or if she's not here, then Marcia's the other senior. We've done out bit; come on, let's have some tea."

***

The staff room was bright and painted a cheerful yellow. Frances took a tea bag from the box and let some hot water from the urn run into a mug. Mavis bustled in as Sylvia opened a tin of biscuits and fetched a pint of milk from the fridge.

"Save me a chocolate one, Sylvie. I need a sugar rush."

Sylvia peered into the tin.

"There's only plain ones left. I'll bring some more tomorrow if there's any money left in the pot. Frances, we all put a fiver in every so often for tea and biscuits."

"Fine." Frances rummaged in her handbag for her purse. "You can have mine now."

"And we cough up every week for a few lines on Euromillions, if you want to join the syndicate?"

"Okay." Frances nodded. "How much?"

"We all pay two pounds fifty except Marcia. So that's me, Mavis, Deana, and a couple of others you haven't met yet, Bernie and Cathy.

Mavis buys the ticket every Friday."

"If you don't pay one week and we win, then you won't get anything." Mavis took a biscuit. "Just making it clear."

"Fair enough; I'll also leave enough money for when I go on holiday." Frances handed over some change to Mavis. "Have you won anything yet?"

"No." Sylvia laughed. "But we live in hope."

Frances smiled at Deana, who appeared in the doorway and glanced her way before making a bolt for the tea urn.

"How's it going, Frances?"

"Okay, I think." Frances moved her legs out of the way so that Deana could pass by. "I was learning the End of Life routine this morning."

"A necessity here I'm afraid, but then again I'm sure you realise that."

"Of course." Frances nodded again. "Sylvie's a good teacher."

"From what I'm hearing, you're doing very well. Keep up the good work."

"Thanks!" Frances sent a beam of appreciation towards Deana. "After being made redundant at the hospital and then not working for a while, I'm a bit nervous."

"Have you *got* to work then, like me?" Sylvia sipped her tea. "I'm divorced and my ex is on the dole."

"Not exactly…" Frances suddenly felt all eyes upon her. "Er…I just like to be occupied all day. The kids have left home, and I'm at a loose end."

"Lucky old you." Mavis chuckled. "How long have you been married then?"

Frances could sense an increased attentiveness from her colleagues, and replied in a neutral tone to try and deflect the interest.

"Thirty five years. How about you?"

"We've just had our silver anniversary. Wow! I bet you're still in love!"

"Oh yes." Frances forced a smile that did not quite reach her eyes. "We're still finding out new things about each other every day."

"He sounds dreamy." Sylvia's cackle echoed around the room. "I should have met him before I shacked up with my ex."

As Frances made her way to the sink to wash up her cup, she inwardly agreed wholeheartedly with her new-found friend.

CHAPTER 15

She hid her surprise at the delicious smell of frying food that hit her full on as she opened the front door. She kept her expression impassive as she walked into the kitchen to be greeted by the sight of her husband wearing her apron over his working overalls, and smiling at her while sticking a fork into something unmoving in the pan.

"I've not long been in, so I thought I'd get dinner started. I picked up some fillet steaks from the butcher's on the way home. There's some oven chips cooking on the two hundred heat as well."

"Let's have my pinny back; probably would have been a good idea to remove those filthy overalls first though." She marched over and took the fork out of his hand. "Go on; I'll take over. Thanks, but what's brought this on?"

She watched as Martin took off the apron and gave it to her with a grin.

"It's the new me. I'm trying to move somewhere towards the man you thought you'd married all those years ago."

She turned over the steaks, wincing at the amount of oil in the saucepan.

"I've already come to terms with the fact that I married somebody else. By the way, you've got enough oil in here to lubricate the Titanic."

"Just trying to help."

She could sense his disappointment and felt a small stab of guilt.

"Thanks anyway. It's a nice gesture."

She sighed as she followed his retreating back with her gaze. She had no idea whether or not he had finally stopped the porn, and realised that for the rest of her life she was going to have to take his word for it. She poked the steak with the fork in a kind of futile anger; *no way was she going to let herself be taken in again by any more of his lies and excuses! There was always some plot hatching behind his eyes, which were too close together to cause him to be anything other than the secretive and shifty person she had found him out to be.* Her thin lips pursed in a straight line as she remembered past visits to his parents, whom she suspected were both tainted with the same secretive gene. She exhaled forcefully while imagining the pair of them brainwashing their son from an early age to always keep his expression impassive, and to give absolutely nothing away.

***

The television was blaring away to itself, and a row of old ladies sat in front of it staring into space. Frances smiled at Mavis, who was perched on a chair holding a fistful of Blu-tack and yards of silver tinsel.

"Give us a hand, Fran. I'm going to strangle meself in a minute."

Frances laughed.

"It's only December the tenth! Isn't it a bit early for Christmas decorations?"

"The residents love a bit of sparkle. It brightens up their day."

"They can have our artificial tree if they like, as well." Frances glanced over at Mavis and then stuck some tinsel on the wall. "We've got all the decorations too. I can bring it in tomorrow."

Mavis raised one thumb up in the air.

"That'll be great, but…don't *you* want it?"

"We're going to our son's place for Christmas Day and Boxing Day." Frances shrugged. "It'd do better here."

"Well, if you're sure…?" Mavis looked questioningly at Frances.

"Absolutely. I'd rather it was somewhere doing a bit of good than stuck up in our loft."

Mavis climbed down from the chair and surveyed the result of her efforts.

"Some of them do go to relatives at Christmas, but the majority stay here."

"I'll get them to help me decorate it." Frances nodded at Mavis. "We'll have a ball."

"Or a bauble?" Mavis chuckled.

***

To her utter dismay the first thing she saw when she returned home that same evening was the long cardboard box containing the artificial tree sliding gracefully down the stairs to rest at her feet.

"Look out, it's Christmas!" Martin's voice emanated somewhere from the upstairs landing. "I've just got the tree out of the loft. Shall we decorate it together?"

Frances took off her coat and hung it on a peg.

"It's hardly going to be a cosy Christmas cuddled up together by a roaring fire, is it?" She kicked the tree out of the way and made her way upstairs, hiding her guilt with a show of bravado. "What's the point? We're going to Colin's, and anyway, I've promised it to the home now. The old girls are looking forward to it."

Two legs clad in blue jeans dangled out of the loft hatch before the rest of his body followed. She watched Martin climbing down the ladder to meet her.

"Look, I'm really trying. D'you think you can cut me a bit of slack here?"

Frances rolled her eyes to the ceiling.

"If you'd told me what you were planning, I wouldn't have mentioned it to Mavis, but let's face it, I didn't think you'd be spending much time at home. Doesn't old Triple Garage Janet need rodding out or something?"

"No, she's going out with your doctor boyfriend now."

Touche. Frances gave Martin the thinnest smile she could conjure up, and then turned on her heel and went downstairs. The fluorescent light in the kitchen buzzed and spluttered into life. She opened the fridge door, took out two long-dead and defrosted pieces of cod, and sighed.

CHAPTER 16

MARTIN

He lifted a six foot tall Nordic pine into the back of his van, cursing at the branches scratching his hands through the netting. The roots stuck out into the night, causing him to have to tie the back doors together with bungee straps. A light frosting of snow whipped his hair into rats' tails. Already there was a fine carpet of pine needles on the floor of his van.

"Jesus H fuckin' Christ!"

Martin kicked the back doors with one hobnailed boot, brushed the snow off his hair, and hurried to the driver's seat. The topmost branches of the pine were sticking through the torn netting and were now in his left peripheral vision. His hands were numb with cold, his stomach rumbled with hunger, and if truth be told, he felt well and truly lacking in festive Christmas spirit.

He was not able to ascertain her reaction as he stumbled in through the front door, as the tree's bulk was blocking his view. However, he listened carefully to the tone of her voice as he manoeuvred the triffid-like plant through the living room door, and came to the rapid conclusion that it did not take the brains of Lloyd George to imagine the sour look that was accompanying her initial greeting.

"There's pine needles all over my bloody carpet!"

His answer came out in a rush between puffs of exertion.

"That's because this is a real tree, not some stupid plastic one."

"I don't want a real tree in my front room! It makes too much mess!"

An absent aroma of something that should have been cooking tipped him right over the edge. He flung the tree downwards. As it hit the Axminster, he took a macabre delight in a fresh shower of needles surrounding the outline of the tree, much like a line of chalk the police might draw around a dead body.

"Chuck it out then! I'm going up for a wash. Is there any dinner?"

"No."

He thought her voice sounded rather too pleased about that fact. "Why not?"

"I've just come in from work, like *you* have."

He shot a parting barb over his shoulder as he made his way back upstairs.

"As far as I can see, your job's doing nothing for our relationship!"

"And neither is your porn addiction!"

Ouch; he had left himself wide open for that one. Martin sighed and stomped up to the bathroom, ignoring another vituperative attack from the ground floor.

"And just because your dinner's not on the table like it used to be, there's no reason to have a childish tantrum!"

He slammed the bathroom door and divested himself of his work clothes, dropping them anywhere except into the dirty laundry basket. He ran hot water into the tub and made sure he used up the last of the bubble bath. Closing his eyes and laying back in the water, his nostrils detected a faint essence of frying sausages.

***

He had no idea why he'd installed a dishwasher; they never seemed to use it. Hands dripping with soapsuds, he passed her the frying pan to dry up.

"Thanks for that dinner; it's always been my favourite."

She took the pan and shrugged.

"That's okay."

Stuffed full of sausage, egg, chips and beans, Martin wanted to wrap himself around her and bury his head in her warm, soft neck.

"I'll get rid of the tree in a minute. I just thought you might like a real one for a change."

The frying pan, unlike the rest of the crockery, failed to make even a dull thud as she placed it carefully on the worktop.

"No, don't chuck it out. See if you can find the box of decorations in the loft that the boys made at school. We can use those, and there must be a spare set of lights up there as well somewhere."

He pulled the plug out of the sink and thanked his lucky stars.

"Richie was always more embarrassed about those decorations than Colin, probably because his spelling was so bad."

He was unaccountably pleased to hear her low chuckle.

"Yeah, remember the bell-shaped thing with 'For my butiful mumy' on it?"

"Poor sod; he was only about seven." Martin wiped his hands on a towel. "Colin took the piss out of it for years." He gave her a tender look. "He had the right idea though."

"As the poem goes, age has withered and the years condemned." She took off her apron and made her way out of the kitchen. "You'll need to find a bucket and fill it up with soil."

"Yes ma'am." Martin was suddenly filled with tentative seasonal joy. "I'm on my way."

***

He knew what would happen as soon as she saw her babies' handiwork of long ago. As he had expected, out came the tissues, and she was dabbing at her eyes even as she took the first decoration out of the box to inspect.

"I can still see Colin striding out of school proudly holding this up to show me. He was seven."

He took a quick look at a well-thumbed crinkled piece of green paper cut in the crude shape of a Christmas tree, with four gold coloured but now slightly detached stars stuck to it.

"After twenty five years our Col probably doesn't even remember making it." He shrugged and rammed the tree stump into the bottom of the bucket, and trod down the earth with his foot. "He's a fella. Us blokes don't get sentimental about things like that."

"Well *I* do." Frances sniffed. "It takes me back to a happier time, when I wasn't searching out porn every single day."

"Do we have to bring porn into every facet of our conversations?" Martin could feel discontent seeping over him. "The porn's gone; you can search until you're blue, but you'll find nothing. That's because *I've- given -it -up*!

He heard a sniff, before the grudging compliance.

"Let's just decorate the tree. I haven't got the energy for yet another argument. Save it 'til tomorrow."

Martin mused that if they could just stay in the same room for even an hour without quarrelling, then he would consider himself a deliriously happy man.

CHAPTER 17

He raised one eyebrow whilst mentally likening her expression to that of somebody suffering from chronic constipation with overflow.

"Would you like to pull my cracker?"

The retort came not from her direction as expected, but from across the table.

"Dad; you say that every year."

Martin fixed his younger son with a haughty gaze.

"Richard Andrews, are you *incinerating* that I'm boring?"

"Yep; and you're mixing up your worms as well."

The wine was helping somewhat in enabling his jolly persona to emerge for a Christmas Day outing. Ignoring her stare of disapproval, he allowed Colin to top up his glass for a fourth time. His gaze roamed benignly around the table at the fruit of his loins, and he enjoyed a brief wave of self-satisfaction before an icy breeze blew in from an easterly direction.

"Colin; no more wine for Dad."

He managed to give Colin a wink without being spotted.

"Lighten up, Mum, it's Christmas. You're driving, yeah?"

"Of course."

Her words were clipped and stentorian. He thought she sounded as though she had a steel rod stuck up her arse.

"Then as long as you're driving, we haven't got to worry, have we?"

Martin knocked back his glass at record speed, but reluctantly put his hand across the rim as Colin uncorked another bottle.

"Any more and I'll be trollied." He slurred. "And then the shit will hit the fan."

He giggled, and caught the eye of his little grandson Charlie, who shot him a wide grin at the same time as his daughter-in-law gave a *tut*.

"Martin, not in front of Charlie, please."

"Sorry Jane."

He couldn't help but giggle at the absurdity of trying to have a merry time whilst sitting beside the Angel of Death, who was obviously hell bent on counting every drink he was managing to pour down his throat. Martin gave a snort of laughter, and two-year old Charlie joined in. He heard Frances give a slight cough before speaking.

"Thanks for putting us up overnight, Col, but we'll be making tracks soon. I'm not keen on driving in the dark."

"We've got the rest of the Christmas pud to get through yet, we didn't finish it yesterday" Jane stood up. "I'll get the brandy and the matches."

He couldn't help himself.

"Just bring the brandy; never mind about the pud!"

He watched Death Angel's grim response, as she flapped her wings in protest while he sat back in his chair and wished he hadn't given up smoking cigars.

***

The house was cold and unwelcoming after a night away. He turned up the thermostat and flopped down onto the settee, nursing a thumping headache. Out of the corner of his eye he watched her bustling about grim-faced, drawing the curtains and switching on the Christmas tree lights. He could not help but think back to their first Christmas; buying presents together wrapped up against the cold, and then afterwards peeling off her layers one by one next to an open fire. He sighed as the exquisite memories came flooding back.

"Serves you right for drinking so much."

Her voice brought him rapidly out of his reverie.

"It's Christmas, fuck it." He rubbed his eyes. "Everybody has a drink at Christmas."

"I don't."

"Perhaps you should." He lay prone on the settee and closed his eyes. "It might loosen you up and bring a smile to your face."

The slamming of the door made him wince. He thought back to a film he couldn't remember the name of. Steve McCroskey, having given up all his addictions, was tearing his hair out in the control tower, while Elaine Dickinson in the aeroplane's cockpit was bending over suggestively inflating the autopilot, a blow-up doll. The autopilot subsequently turned around to the camera with a leer, and Martin laughed to himself at the memory of it and wondered if it was the right time to begin snorting crack cocaine.

***

Just the Christmas tree lights were illuminating the room when he woke up. He sat up, dishevelled, disorientated, and with a raging thirst. He looked at the wall opposite and saw the clock's hands showing a quarter to midnight. Yawning, he got to his feet and made his way towards the kettle and a hot cup of coffee, surprised to find his very own Angel of Death seated at the kitchen table reading from a Kindle.

"I thought you'd be in bed." He yawned again, filled up the kettle, and switched it on. "Want some coffee?"

"If you like. I couldn't sleep."

The angel wings had ceased to flap, and to Martin she looked somehow resigned and demoralised. Deciding to stay silent to avoid a late-night scene which might stop him from sleeping altogether, he padded to the fridge and took out a bottle of milk. He felt her eyes burning into his back as he spooned some coffee into two mugs, and felt compelled to turn around and face her.

"What?" She turned off the Kindle and looked at him.

"Nothing." He shrugged. "Just waiting for the kettle to boil."

"You were pissed earlier at Colin's. You were embarrassing."

He filled up the mugs and handed one over to her.

"I'm going to have a shower, and then I'm going to bed. That's all I've got to say really."

"You never could stand confrontations."

He took a sip of coffee and forced a smile.

"There is no point talking to you. You're convinced I'm a porn-addicted alcoholic. There's nothing I can do or say to convince you I'm now neither of these things, and so I'm not even going to try. You despise me from the depths of your soul, and so I'm going to say goodnight and walk away."

And with these words he turned around and headed out of the door with as much dignity as he could muster.

CHAPTER 18

FRANCES

To Frances, twisting and turning in an effort to sleep, it seemed as though the whole world was rotten to the core. Her husband had been lured away across the Acheron, and had sunk into a kind of Dante's Inferno of depravity. She had no idea why some men got their kicks from watching other people having sex, but what she did know is that she never wanted Martin to get into her bed ever again.

It felt strange not being able to check for evidence on the voice recorder every night before she went to sleep. The listening was like soothing balm, and often she had woken up in the morning with the headphones still on and a low battery signal on the display screen. Now there was nothing to do except to lay there and think about what he was doing in the other room.

He had kept his word and his iPhone had remained on the kitchen table every night. She considered it futile to keep checking through texts and viewing history, as she knew his habit to delete all his messages and websites was too ingrained. Instead, she stared into the blackness and wondered whether he had another phone that she did not know about. She had already found one in the past containing the number of an escort agency he used when away on business trips, and although she had stamped on it in front of him, she was certain that his addiction was such that a secret mobile phone was an absolute necessity.

With a sigh she climbed out of bed and put on her dressing gown and slippers. She reasoned that with the amount of alcohol he had consumed earlier that afternoon, he would now be sleeping like the proverbial log. It was time to search his room.

Loud snoring assailed her ears as soon as she stepped out onto the landing. She dimmed the upstairs light slightly, and inched open his bedroom door. The room smelt musty and faintly of alcohol, and Frances wrinkled her nose. Rays of light illuminated the furniture and the body of the sleeper lying on his right side facing the wall.

She crept over to the bed, sank quietly to her knees, and fished around underneath the bed. She found nothing of note, and so began to crawl around each side of the bed, sticking her arm under the base as far as it would go. There was nothing under there but fluff. The snoring did not change in rate or intensity, and so Frances was emboldened to search the room further.

Standing up stiffly, she cursed the creaking of her dodgy left knee, and moved over towards the chest of drawers nearest the door. Easing open the first drawer she peered inside and riffled through underpants and socks. So intent was she in her quest that she failed to hear a slight cough until it was too late.

"What the fuck are you doing?"

Her heart felt as though it was going to leap out of her chest, as she turned around to see him sitting up and scratching his head. She came up with the only answer she could think of in that split second.

"I'm putting the laundry away."

"At two o'clock in the morning?"

She closed the drawer and damned him to eternity.

"It seemed a good idea at the time."

"I thought you'd come in for a cuddle."

She backed off towards the door.

"Go back to sleep. See you in the morning.

***

She was glad of the excuse to leave for an early morning shift at the home. As soon as he appeared in the kitchen doorway she knew that trouble lay ahead.

"Tell me I was dreaming. Were you in my room last night?"

She turned a few rashers of bacon over in the frying pan and kept her back to him.

"I told you. I was putting the washing away."

She concentrated on frying the bacon, inwardly shivering on becoming aware that he had stepped in closer and was now almost breathing down her neck.

"It takes a liar to know a liar. What were you looking for?"

She jumped into a pregnant pause with both feet, and moved the frying pan away from the heat source.

"Ah, so at last you admit that you've been lying to me!"

"Don't change the subject." He shook his head. "If you tell me what you were looking for, then perhaps I can help you find it."

She turned around to face him.

"Okay! If you really must know, I was looking around to see if you had another mobile phone hidden away somewhere, like last time."

She could tell by the expression on his face that he was trying too hard to control his anger.

"There's no let up with you is there? You just *don't* give me a break!"

She drained the bacon and sighed as she buttered some bread and cut a round of sandwiches.

"There's no let up because you've let me down so often. Perhaps try and see things from my point of view for a change."

He poured out two mugs of tea, then took a sandwich from the plate and sat down.

"Yes I know what I've done to you, but you've got to put it to the back of your mind and move on, otherwise we're never going to get back to normal. Whatever I did in the past, I've stopped doing it now. I don't know what else I can do to make you believe me."

She ate absent-mindedly and sipped her tea, trying not to look at him chewing mournfully. At length she stood and picked up her bag, and felt like ramming all the rest of the sandwiches down his throat at once.

"I'll leave you to clear up. My shift starts in half an hour."

***

Mavis and Sylvia were still wearing Santa hats. Frances acknowledged Bernie Price as he waved to her whilst cleaning a commode.

"Good Christmas Fran?"

"Lovely, thanks." Frances sent him a beaming smile. "How about you?"

"Oh, the usual. I help out down at the homeless shelter on Market Street. Now Mum's gone it gives me something to do, and I enjoy it."

She took a quick glance at the bare third finger of his left hand. She had imagined Bernie sitting in his front room at Christmas surrounded by a clutch of children and grandchildren."

"Oh, sorry, I didn't realise you'd been on your own."

"Why should you?" Bernie smiled and washed his hands. "Anyway, I have a great time at the shelter. There's always a party atmosphere down there at Christmas, and Easter too."

"Maybe I should try it as well." Frances replied with interest.

"I've only been doing it for a couple of years, but it grows on you. I couldn't imagine ever doing anything else on Christmas Day now."

As she buttoned up her overall, Frances warmed to her new work colleague, and came to the rapid conclusion that anything would be better than spending another Christmas or Easter with her absolute pig of a husband.

CHAPTER 19

MARTIN

The knowledge that she had been ferreting about in his bedroom at night was enough to send a stab of fear shooting through his heart. As soon as she had left for work, Martin carried a toolbox up to his bedroom and set about installing a lock. When he had successfully tested out the new key he stepped back with a grin on his face, added the key to the bunch he already had, and let a certain amount of satisfaction seep over his features at the result of his handiwork. He sighed; the relief at now being able to sleep in peace was overwhelming.

He was certain that she would never find exactly what she was looking for, because only *he* knew where it was. Grinning, he took a crowbar out of his toolbox, pushed his bed to one side, and lifted up a corner of the carpet. He hadn't used the phone for months, but there it still was, gathering dust underneath the floorboards. He took the phone out of its cloth cover, all the while resisting the temptation to charge it up and call Heidi at the escort agency one more time.

Heidi was the most polite Madam he had ever had the good fortune to contact. Not only did she treat all paying customers with the utmost respect, she also demanded the same respect for her girls, who were all above average intelligence, certifiably clean, and eager to please. However, with a twinge of regret Martin knew he had to consign the phone and his previous lifestyle to the rubbish bin for even a slim chance of winning back his rightful place in his wife's affections.

The sledgehammer made short work of the phone out in the back garden. He made sure he swept up every last shard, and then purposely emptied the kitchen bin and added a new liner, before dropping the mangled remains of the phone into the clean bin. The removal of the last remnant of his previous life left him feeling strangely free and whole again. He packed up his tools, and even a day to be spent on a freezing cold building site failed to dampen his spirits. As he left the house, he was whistling.

***

He waited for the inevitable inquisition over dinner, which she managed to save until they had attacked the last of the apple crumble.

"I couldn't help but notice the mangled phone in the bin."

He swallowed the last mouthful and leaned back in his seat.

"You were supposed to. I saved you the trouble of another sleepless night turning my room upside down."

Her face took on that self-righteous expression that he knew so well.

"I thought you said you didn't have a phone earlier on."

"No, I didn't say that, but I did stop using it a while back. I chucked it out this morning, as you saw."

He knew she would milk the subject until the bitter end.

"How do I know you haven't got another one?"

He shrugged.

"You don't. You'll have to take my word for it."

"Your *word?*" She hooted with laughter. "That's rich!"

He stood up, suddenly sick to death of it all.

"I've put a lock on my bedroom door. It doesn't mean I'm shutting you out because I've got another woman in there or because I'm sending secret text messages, it's just because I want an undisturbed night's sleep. I'm going down the pub. Not to get bladdered, just to have a pint in an atmosphere that's somewhat less frosty than this one."

He didn't even wait to see her reaction, but turned around and headed straight for the front door, slamming it behind him with great force and satisfaction.

***

He acknowledged the landlord's wave by raising his hand.

"Hi Rob." Martin perched on one of the high bar stools. "Good Christmas?"

The landlord rolled his eyes towards the ceiling.

"We were busy Christmas Day with the dinners. We were so knackered afterwards that we fell asleep and missed most of it! How about you?"

"Fuckin' awful." Martin laughed. "Give us a pint of your best, ta."

The beer tasted good after a dry week trying to convince his wife that he wasn't an alcoholic. From his vantage point Martin looked around the bar at the few people dotted about, who were sitting slumped in a kind of post-festive fug.

"Quiet in here tonight." He took another gulp of beer. "Your roast turkey must have given them all the shits."

"Bloody cheek." Rob Guthrie polished a glass and grinned. "The beer's a bit buggy though, just in case you need a clear out."

"Nah, I'm an expert." Martin held his glass up to the light. "Nothing wrong with this nectar, mate."

"So…" Rob yawned. "What will two thousand and fourteen have in store for you?"

"God knows." Martin shrugged. "A trip down Bourbon Street in New Orleans; *that* I know for certain. But apart from the holiday, I'm just taking it one day at a time."

CHAPTER 20

FRANCES

In the past she had been able to throw anything into Martin's case that hadn't managed to fit into hers. Now she was locked out and no more could she simply waltz in and hide a few evening dresses or a pair of sandals under his shirts. Frances kicked the bedroom door in anger, which still steadfastly refused to budge. She would have to jettison some of the contents of her case instead, which was four kilogrammes over the regulation limit.

As Martin's key turned in the front door, Frances retreated into her room. She heard footsteps run up the stairs and the sound of a key unlocking the door that had so recently mocked her futile attempts at entry. Aware that he had walked across the landing and was now threatening to invade her personal space, she ensured she kept her back to him.

"Hi, I've finished work for two weeks now. I'm in holiday mode!"

His voice sounded overly cheerful, and she wanted to scream.

"I'm just doing some packing."

"Feel free to add anything to my case. I expect yours is over the limit?"

She hid a small smile before answering in a dull monotone.

"Cheers."

She tried to ignore his ritual throat clearing.

"I'm setting my alarm for half four, Fran. Shall I come in and wake you up?"

"No."

"We'll get to Heathrow with plenty of time. Did you check on the terminal?"

She nodded.

"Three. All flights with Virgin go from terminal three."

"Okay then. What's for dinner?"

She threw a pair of sandals at him and he caught them deftly.

"I'm in holiday mode as well. There isn't any."

"Great. I'll go down the chippy then."

"Haddock and chips for me please." She zipped up her case and checked the label. "With a couple of big gherkins on the side."

"Coming up!" He gave a mock salute whilst holding both sandals in his left hand. "I'll be back quick as a flash!"

***

She was so hungry that she could not even be bothered to put the fish and chips on a plate. She took the hot, aromatic parcel of food from him and sat down at the kitchen table, picking up a chip straight from the paper with her fingers.

"At least I won't have to cook for the next two weeks."

He sat down beside her with his own meal and peeled back a layer of greaseproof paper.

"We won't have to do anything except get to know each other again."

She picked out a piece of flaky fish and popped it into her mouth.

"I already know you. That's the problem."

"You knew the *old* me." He waggled a chip at her. "This time there's a new Martin Andrews trying to make himself heard."

"Tell me something worth listening to then." She sighed.

"Okay I will." He munched on the chip before it fell from his hand. "Let's call a truce and begin from scratch, shall we? We've a lovely holiday coming up. Perhaps it's time we started again. What do you say Fran?"

"Time will tell whether or not you're a changed man." She shrugged. "But I'm willing to try and enjoy the holiday at least. That's all I can say."

"Then that's good enough for me." He smiled at her. "Can I have one of your gherkins?"

***

As soon as she could after take-off, Frances donned some headphones and turned on the in-flight entertainment screen, smiling as she saw one of the movie options was the thinking-woman's hunk Colin Firth in *Genius*, which she decided to watch rather than listening to Martin's inane chatter. Purposely closing herself off to communication, and with the elderly American woman next to him asleep, from her peripheral vision she noticed her husband idly leafing through the safety brochure and then opening a plastic bag containing headphones in order to listen to some AC/DC.

So engrossed in the film did she become, that when Max Perkins asked Thomas Wolfe if he had ever looked in anybody's eyes and *ached*, she had to look out of the window to compose herself. *Yes*, she had ached for her babies, and for Martin at the start of their marriage, but more recently it had been just for *Graham*, a futile unrequited ache that never seemed to go away.

"I wouldn't feed this to a dog."

A nudge to her arm brought her out of her reverie. She caught Martin's look of contempt as he gazed down at a steaming silver container of sausages and lentils swimming in a thin gravy. She grimaced as he took a second covered container from the stewardess and pushed it in her direction.

"Thanks. I think."

"Eat up. Good thing we're near the toilets."

***

The coach headed north out of Miami airport for some miles on the Interstate 95 expressway carrying its cargo of excited cruise passengers. Frances gazed out of the window and thought of Graham, whilst enjoying a view of golf courses and palm trees swaying in the hot afternoon sunshine. Beside her she heard Martin yawn and fumble through a sheaf of paperwork while the coach rumbled along the Ives Dairy Road and Aventura Boulevard, eventually coming to a halt on West Country Club Drive opposite the Safra Bank of New York. She looked around her, perplexed, and felt a stab of irritation as she heard his chuckle.

"Did I tell you we're not boarding the ship until tomorrow morning? You haven't seemed that interested, but the coach is taking us to a hotel first; we've got an overnight stay."

Frances suffered a sudden heartsink moment at the implication of his statement.

***

"Are they all Michael Jackson fans, or what?"

She stepped out onto the balcony and followed Martin's gaze past a row of buggies with their bags of golf clubs on the back, towards several men as they stood chatting on an expanse of green lawn stretching off into the distance.

"What're you talking about?

"Their hands, look. All the golfers are only wearing one glove on their left hand."

"Perhaps they're going to moonwalk around the course. By the way, I'm having the bed on the left."

"Sure, whatever." He shrugged. "Sorry, I didn't know the hotel was full. D'you think the golf shop downstairs might have a big box of right handed gloves for sale?"

Frances hid a grin and looked up to watch a group of buzzards circling overhead.

"Perhaps they all have eczema on one hand and feel embarrassed. There's no kettle, so it's coffee or nothing."

"Don't Americans drink tea then?" He looked towards her.

"How do I know?" She rubbed her eyes. "I've never been here before."

"Did you see the prices on the menu? Good job we're only staying one night."

***

She took her time, luxuriating in the kind of hot bath one can only enjoy after a nine hour flight. Steadfast in her resolve to keep her husband at arm's length, she endured a strained dinner, inwardly screaming at his constant grumbling about prices, and begged an early night. Despite the unfamiliar surroundings, she was surprised to awaken at 6am after a sound sleep by lawn mowers trundling up and down the green outside, together with the noise of buggies pulling rakes across the sand bunkers. She looked across to where Martin slept on unconcerned in the middle of a queen-sized bed, and wondered what the coming fortnight would bring.

***

Mid-morning the coach carried on along the Interstate 95 freeway towards Fort Lauderdale, and Frances began to notice signs indicating that Port Everglades was approaching. From the tone of his replies to the couple across the aisle, Martin was hiding an ennui she recognised so well. She hoped they wouldn't be stuck with the middle-aged pair going on about their previous Caribbean cruise for the rest of the holiday, and decided to keep her head down in her novel.

"Christ! That's a big bugger!"

She looked up from her Kindle at Martin's exclamation to see *The Majestyk*, a towering white edifice blocking the horizon in Berth 18 as the coach came to a stop. Craning her neck upwards she could see many orange lifeboats on launching frames hanging in a long line across the middle of the ship, and at least another 10 decks rising above those, from where passengers looked down at the coach from their balconies and clapped to a bead-wearing jazz band playing on the dock.

"Oh!" She was temporarily at a loss for words.

"Let's get off this coach before I strangle Ethel and Walter." Martin hissed into her ear. "If I hear about their Cayman Islands' ride of death in a tender once more, then I won't be responsible for my actions."

Once safely through Customs and armed with their shiny new Seapass cards, Frances followed behind Martin as he eschewed the ship's lifts with their long line of elderly and disabled passengers queuing patiently, and took the stairs up to the Ocean View café on deck 14. She hoped his legs would cramp at the exertion and he would have to stop, but he was in fine fettle and buoyed up for the holiday. She arrived at the top of the ship red-faced and panting, and ignored him pointedly performing a few quadriceps stretches while he waited for her to catch up.

"Next time I'm going in the lift."

"It's the only exercise we'll get for a fortnight; the gym will be full of grunters in Speedos." He shrugged. "Come on, let's get some lunch."

***

The buffet was full of newbies clutching plates and walking dazedly around various food outlets. Far down on the dock below she could see more coaches unloading their human cargo. Frances ate a ham salad and looked out of the window enviously at young-at-heart couples walking arm-in-arm into Customs, and ensured her eyes remained averted from her husband as he demolished a pungent plate of chicken curry and chips.

"This is the life. The cabins are on deck seven; we can find them in a minute. Are you having dessert?"

"No." Frances shook her head and nibbled on a breadstick. "If I start that, my clothes won't fit."

"Live dangerously; I'll buy you some bigger ones."

"Actually I'm done. I'm going down to find my cabin now, and see if my luggage has arrived.

"Okay, I'll give you a knock in a while. I'm next door, so when we've unpacked perhaps we can go and sit by the pool?"

"If you like."

She left him filling up with ice cream, and found the stairs again to deck 7. Cabin assistants were running to and fro depositing suitcases, and she was pleased to discover her luggage was already outside her door. As soon as she had inserted her Seapass card into the lock and turned on the light, her eyes came to rest straight away on an inter-connecting door standing wide open. With a start she rushed towards it and rammed home the bolt.

CHAPTER 21

MARTIN

He checked the inter-connecting door to her cabin, but she had either locked it or it had never been opened in the first place. Martin sighed with disappointment and prepared himself for her disapproval of the secret plan he had engineered with the travel agent all those months ago. He slumped onto the bed and grabbed the TV remote switch on the bedside table just as the phone rang.

"You never told me you'd booked cabins with an inter-connecting door."

The tone of her voice told Martin that he had better come up with a good answer.

"I didn't. The travel agent must have done it."

"Pull the other one."

"It's true." He lied and switched on the TV. "What number did you use to call my cabin?"

"The instructions are on your phone, but you just put a nine in front of the cabin number. Have you got your luggage yet?"

"No." He felt relieved that the topic had moved on. "How about you?"

"Yeah, mine's here. I'm unpacking."

"Give me a ring when you've finished, and we can have a walk round."

"Okay."

He fell back against the pillow and flicked through the channels. An over-made up young woman tried to entice him into buying another cruise holiday. He gazed at the pert outline of her breasts and cursed his weakness for the female form.

***

As far as he could tell, he and Fran seemed to be the youngest people on the ship. He looked away with distaste at the flabby flesh on display around the pool.

"Jeez; I never knew they made bikinis that big."

It pleased him to realise she was trying not to smile as she focused on her novel, and he let his eyes linger for a fraction on her still-slim legs in their khaki shorts before settling further down on the sun lounger and closing his eyes.

"No cozzie then?"

"No." She shook her head. "Nobody needs to see me in a swimming costume, especially *you.*"

The scathing *you* made him bite back the complimentary retort.

"I'll have a dip in a minute. Arnel delivered my stuff, but I haven't unpacked it all yet."

"Knowing you, you probably won't."

"I'm a changed man; even my tee-shirts will be colour coordinated in the wardrobe."

"They're all black."

"Well, some are light black and some are dark black."

He used to love making her laugh. Her laughter always told him that all was right in her world. Now her nose was too frequently immersed in a Kindle, and she tried to hide the fact that she found his remarks funny. He felt at a loss for what to do to please her.

Noise levels increased as one of the entertainment staff switched on a PA system and encouraged line dancers to step forward. Martin gave up trying to doze, and sat up.

"Some of these whelks need to move a bit."

He caught her eye as she looked up.

"Are you talking about the pregnant men?"

"Could be." He chuckled. "The brochure showed young, tanned people in their twenties sitting around a pool. Man, I think we're on the wrong ship."

He watched her eyes making a quick panoramic sweep.

"Most of these men are well past their due date."

"I'm glad you kept *your* figure." He grinned. "I'm going for a swim."

He stood up, kicked off his crocs, made sure his trunks were tied, and walked over to the pool. He could sense her staring at his back as he hurriedly lifted his feet off the hot ground, and was doubly glad he hadn't let himself go. He raised his arms, curled his toes around the edge of the pool, took a deep breath, and dived in.

The water was refreshing against the heat of the afternoon. Martin was pleased to have the pool to himself, and swam a few lengths in long, practised strokes. He floated for a while on his back, and then hauled himself out and flopped back dripping onto the sun lounger.

"You can still dive then."

Her voice was teasing and unusually light-hearted. He felt pleased that she had been watching.

"Just about, *and* I can haul myself out without a hoist."

"Aren't *you* the clever one?"

He grinned at her and felt *The Majestyk's* engines start up far below them.

"We're off. Next stop Georgetown in two days' time. Arnel told me there are four engines although there's mostly only two being used, and each engine burns ten tonnes of fuel every hour. The cruise will use up over a million dollars in fuel. He's a little mine of information."

"Blimey; no wonder they charge so much for the cabins."

He rubbed his chest dry with a towel, and considered with relish one of their first conversations in months that had not ended with an argument.

CHAPTER 22

He rapped on the inter-connecting door, which still refused to yield under pressure.

"You ready? They're calling us to the tenders on Channel 6."

After hearing her muffled reply, Martin grabbed his camera and waited out in the corridor. He thought she looked particularly pretty that afternoon in purple shorts and a white tee-shirt, but refrained from being too effusive about her appearance.

"Hi. All set?"

"Yes, despite the slight rocking from side to side." She grimaced. "Can you feel it?"

"Yeah, it's a bit windy. I think there's a storm forecast for later on today, but hopefully we'll be back on the ship by then."

"I hope so."

They moved along the corridor and took the stairs down to the gangway on deck two, joining the end of a queue of exiting passengers waiting to have their Seapass cards scanned. An open tender bobbed gracefully on the water outside the gangway. Martin helped Frances into the tender, and sat down.

"At least the wind's dying down now."

"Hmm." She sounded unconvinced.

He was pleased for Frances that the crossing was not too rough.

An open sided trolley-bus waited for them on Georgetown pier. Martin grabbed an outer seat next to Frances, and wondered briefly if there would be time for a snifter on the way back in 'The Rum Stop' that he had spied opposite. He listened with half an ear to the driver's well-rehearsed monologue as the trolley rumbled off, trying not to stare at a young woman's shiny blonde hair hanging down over the back of the seat in front.

"Wow, imagine no taxes apart from when you buy a house, and there's over six hundred banks on the island and it's only twenty two miles wide!"

Frances was obviously giving the driver her full attention. Martin was happy she was speaking to him at all, and took a couple of desultory snaps of millionaire's houses as they trundled along.

"What a good idea, burying rellies in front of their homes."

"I wouldn't like that." Frances shuddered. "Oh, it's started to rain."

Martin looked up; the sky had darkened considerably. The rain began to fall down in huge drops, soaking through his clothes and making him feel somewhat pissed off. As far as he was concerned, The Rum Stop beckoned. The trolley pulled off the main road, and the driver unrolled long, opaque plastic sheeting down the sides. Beside him, Frances grumbled.

"Now I can't see anything."

Martin wanted to laugh at the state of the couple who had raced to bag the front seats. They were now thoroughly drenched, and were looking hopefully behind them with long faces.

A torrent of rain made any more sightseeing impossible, and the driver returned to the pier. Martin pointed past kiosks selling souvenirs towards The Green Parrot bar.

"Let's run over there and wait for the next tender!"

After a couple of beers he felt more affable.

"The last tender goes in twenty minutes." Frances glanced at her watch. "It's still raining."

Martin shrugged.

"We'll have to get it then, or the ship will go without us."

Reluctantly they made their way to where the last tender heaved and rolled on the waves. A queue had formed to board, and waves washed over their shoes. Without umbrellas they were soon soaked.

"My trainers are squelching!"

Martin looked at Frances' pale face and then down at her shoes, and had a sudden ominous dread about the return journey in the pit of his stomach. The line of passengers moved forward onto the tender, and he looked about for two empty seats.

"Let's sit here in the middle. It might not rock so much."

"I don't want to do this." Frances voice trembled. "I want to go back to the pier."

"We can't." He stroked her hair. "This is the last tender of the afternoon."

The little boat pulled away as the wind speed and driving rain increased the size of the waves, to loud cheers from the passengers. Martin knew that Frances' silence had nothing to do with him, and he put a reassuring arm around her shoulders. He tied the camera around his neck, felt her lean into him, and there and then thanked the Lord for the storm.

A cheer and a *Mexican Wave* from several soaking wet passengers in the front seats accompanied each roll of the boat in the ten foot high waves. The engine strained as the tender pursued its torturous journey towards the ship. Martin held his wife close, and tried to ignore the sound of a woman emptying her stomach contents into a plastic bag on the other side of the aisle. He looked down at Frances, who had her eyes closed.

He could see the huge hull of *The Majestyk* approaching and three officers standing on one of the gangways ready to receive them. Cruise passengers were enjoying the drama from the safety of their balconies, some leaning over as far as they could to get a better view. Martin felt like making a V sign, but cuddled Frances closer instead.

As well as rolling up and down in the heavy sea, the tender now began to rock violently from side to side and bash against the hull of the ship, jolting the terrified passengers about in their seats. Martin was no sailor, but he knew that the tender would never be able to dock. One of the crew started to hand out life jackets, and another took down a long pole with a hook on one end which was attached to the ceiling of the tender and instead placed it on the floor. Passengers in the front seats stopped waving their arms in unison and fell silent.

Martin could hear his wife crying silent tears of hopelessness. He took the life jackets that were handed to him and helped his wife on with hers, but decided he could manage to keep her alive longer without the constraints of a huge orange buoyancy aid around his neck. A burst of adrenaline kept him alert, and he wiped salty water from his eyes and lips. He whispered into the wet strands of Frances' hair.

"If we go in the water I'll keep you afloat, don't worry. We're near the ship, we won't drown."

Her reply was lost over the roar of the engine and he held her close, enjoying the feel of her arms around his waist. Martin heard the captain shouting to officers on the gangway that the tender would return to the pier to be exchanged for a bigger vessel. He never wanted to let Frances go, and he buried his face in the top of her head, enjoying the unexpected and welcome closeness all the way back to the shore.

A larger tender had materialised by the time they reached the pier. He could see that Frances was so shaky she could barely stand, and he supported her with one arm around her waist.

"Hey, you're Mrs Wet Tee Shirt two thousand and fourteen."

He was rewarded with a faint smile as they stood on the jetty. Twenty five soaking wet and silent passengers boarded *The Carib Lady* just as the rain stopped and the sun peeped out from behind the clouds. As they docked safely next to *The Majestyk*, officers and crew handed out blankets and steaming cups of hot chocolate. He watched Frances handing over her Seapass and being wrapped up and fussed over in the gangway, and wondered how on earth he could have carried on without her.

CHAPTER 23

He stepped out of the shower, dried himself off and put on the dressing gown provided, trying not to show his surprise on exiting the bathroom and finding his wife sitting waiting patiently on the settee. The inter-connecting door was wide open, and he noticed Frances had now dressed herself in dry clothing and had re-styled her hair.

"Okay now?"

He looked her up and down. Colour had returned to her cheeks, and as far as he could tell she looked none the worse for their adventure.

"I don't know. All I do know is that I never want to go on a tender again. We should have listened to Ethel and Walter."

"Who?" He looked at her quizzically.

"Those two bores on the coach the other day. Weren't they talking about a ride of death in the Cayman Islands?"

"They might have been." He shrugged his shoulders. "I wasn't really listening."

"I had a message on my phone." She pointed towards his bedside table. "You've probably got the same one. There's a red light flashing."

He picked up the phone and pressed the button to retrieve messages.

"Somebody from Guest Services." He replaced the receiver. "Apologising for the incident and asking if there's anything they can do for me."

"Same as mine." Frances nodded. "Perhaps they're frightened we're going to sue."

"Well, I might." Martin mused. "It's not something people want to go through on their holiday."

"I heard the *Majestyk*'s officers telling a passenger that they weren't our ship's tenders." Frances stated quietly. "They'd hired a local fleet."

"Someone's cocked up." Martin combed his hair and sat down beside her. "We might be able to play this to our advantage."

He was enjoying the relaxed atmosphere between them. For once they were not discussing his shortcomings, and now they had a totally new shared experience to talk about. Martin was not altogether sorry that the incident had taken place.

"How?" Frances turned to face him.

"Remember that tour of the galley, the navigational bridge, the laundry and the engine control room that you wanted to do but it was too expensive? We could ask Guest Services if we could go on that for free for our trouble."

"They'd never agree." Frances shook her head. "They'd lose out on two hundred pounds."

"I'll go downstairs and speak to them." Martin pulled out clean but crumpled pants, shorts and a tee shirt from his case. "If we don't ask we'll never know."

He decided to throw caution to the wind and take off his dressing gown. Naked, he hopped onto one foot and then the other to don boxer shorts, whilst noticing out of the corner of his eye Frances standing up and making for the inter-connecting door.

"I'll come with you." She tossed the remark over her shoulder before stepping through the door and locking it gently. "I'll just get my bag and then wait for you in the corridor."

***

Martin brandished two tickets around in the air with a triumphant grin.

"It always pays to ask."

With difficulty Frances kept up with her husband as he strode up the stairs to the Ocean View Cafe.

"You had a bit of a cheek asking for a free cruise next year though."

He chuckled.

"I thought it best to test out just *how* eager they were to make amends."

Frances found herself panting again as they reached deck 14.

"Now we'll be forever earmarked as those greedy, grasping Brits."

"Nah." Martin shook his head and held open the door of the café. "Every single one of them on that tender will be after all they can get."

CHAPTER 24

FRANCES

At least this time she was not adrift on a raging sea. Frances, trying to prise apart her too-tight lifejacket a little bit, stepped down into the dolphin pool behind Martin.

"I didn't think I'd be wearing this bloody thing again quite so soon." She hissed.

Two grey streaks flashed past her as she trod warily along a platform through chest-deep water towards a trainer blowing short, sharp bursts on his whistle. Two sleek heads emerged inches from where she had come to a stop, hugging the wall.

"Now Martin and Fran, step forward, hold up your hands, and wave. Netty and Anya will wave back."

Feeling a little foolish with sightseers gawping from the railings above, Frances copied Martin and held up the palms of both hands, waggling them about for extra effect. She could not help but grin at the sight of two dolphins rising out of the water and moving their fins in unison at them, before expertly catching a fishy reward from their trainer.

"Now hold out your hands, palms downwards. Netty and Anya will swim underneath and you can pet them as they go past. Steer clear of their blowholes though."

Frances grinned at Martin, who she could see was enjoying himself just as much as she was. She was amazed at how smooth the dolphins felt as they swam under her hands.

"Which one of you would like to kiss Anya?"

She heard Martin snort.

"I ain't kissing no dolphin."

She giggled and raised an arm, feeling somewhat emboldened.

"I will."

"Anya will come up to you." The trainer blew a whistle. "Put one hand on the end of her nose and look up while our photographer takes a snap, and then put both hands under her mouth and give her a kiss."

Frances giggled at the photographer, not used to being up so close and personal to a dolphin. When her lips met the rubbery feel of Anya's, she heard the crowd above clapping and her husband roaring with laughter. She felt good, and wanted to wrap her arms around Anya and give her a hug.

"Now here's something Martin can do." The trainer lobbed some fish in Anya's direction and made a sign to Netty. "See how far you can throw this ring across the pool for Netty to retrieve."

"Yep, I can do that." Martin nodded. "Chuck it over here, mate."

When the quoit-like ring left Martin's hand, Frances watched it soar straight across to the other side of the pool.

"Get that, Netty!"

The dolphin was gone in a silent, sleek dive. Frances clapped as seconds later it emerged with the ring on the end of its nose, presenting it to the trainer in reward for a mouthful of fish.

"Fancy a ride on a boogie board?"

The trainer was watching both of them for a reply. Frances shook her head and hugged the wall again, but was surprised when her husband raised his hand.

"Sounds good!"

"Okay." The trainer blew his whistle and grabbed a boogie board from the side of the pool. "Martin, lie face down on this board, and you'll see what Netty can do."

Frances raised her thumb at Martin and received a leery wink. She was not prepared for the speed at which the board and Martin arrived at the other side of the pool, and was glad she had declined the trainer's offer.

"Wow!" Martin exclaimed after swimming back a few moments after Netty had already swallowed a handful of fish. "That was awesome! Have a go, Fran!"

"Er… I'm happy watching, thanks." She shook her head.

"One last photo." The trainer signalled to the dolphins and the photographer. "Martin, put your arm around your lovely wife, and your other arm around Anya."

Frances once again felt Martin's arm around her, and leaned in towards him. His body felt so familiar, and yet so much had happened to tear them apart. As she stood there smiling inanely, all she could think about was how many women her husband's arms might have enveloped over the previous thirty five years. She did not trust him one iota, and that was the root of their problem which would never go away no matter how much he wanted it to. The damage was done.

"You'll be able to collect your photos from the ticket office in about half an hour." The trainer signalled to the next couple to step down into the water. "I hope you enjoyed your time with us."

Frances stepped out of the pool and smiled at the photographer.

"How much are the photos?"

"Thirty dollars each, Madam."

"I think we'll be leaving it, thanks." Martin gave the photographer a stare.

"Oh come on Martin." Frances took off her lifejacket. "Let's get the one of us with Anya. We'll probably never do anything like this ever again."

"I hate being ripped off." Martin threw his lifejacket onto the pile. "But if it's what you want, then I'll get it for you."

"Yeah." Frances waved farewell to the trainer. "It's what I want."

CHAPTER 25

She eschewed a trip with Martin to San Miguel, wanting a morning to herself to be primped, pampered and powdered at the ship's hairdressing and fitness salon, and then to sit on the top deck alone with her Kindle. Frances sensed her husband's disappointment as she waved him goodbye and made her way to deck 12. She felt smothered by his attentions, and needed some breathing space.

There appeared to be no other passengers needing a facial, manicure or a new hair style, and Frances revelled in being the hairdressing salon's sole customer. Three hours later she stretched out on a lounger in the sun and felt relaxed, rejuvenated, and twenty years younger. She picked up her Kindle and sighed with contentment.

After about fifteen minutes she was jolted out of her reverie by a deep voice emanating from above her head.

"Has anybody claimed this seat?"

Frances looked up to see an overweight middle-aged man wearing just swimming shorts pointing to the only other unoccupied sun lounger next to hers. She nodded.

"Yes, it's my husband's when he returns from San Miguel. They're on their way back now I think."

"Oh well, I'll take it for now then if I may. My wife went on that trip too. I didn't fancy it. I'm Desmond, but you can call me Des."

She felt a brief wave of irritation flash over her as the man made himself comfortable, spreading out a towel and plonking himself down beside her with much heaving and grunting. Once settled, she was aware that his eyes were focused on her.

"Good book?"

She looked across at Desmond's huge girth spreading out over the sides of the sun lounger, and thought him not unlike a beached whale.

"Yeah." She nodded. "It's called No Sex Please, I'm Menopausal!"

She turned back to her Kindle, and heard him let out a snort of laughter.

"Not much of a read then?"

Frances checked her watch.

"On the contrary, it's very funny. It's about this arsehole of a man who thinks he's God's gift to women, and who finally learns a lesson."

She was not going to let him get the better of her nor make her give up her prize position on the top deck. She sat up and swivelled her legs to one side so that she had her back to him.

"My wife went off sex years ago."

Frances began to boil with suppressed rage. Turning just her neck, she glanced over her shoulder.

"Perhaps getting into bed with you wasn't doing it for her."

She was suddenly aware that her replies were having a galvanising effect on Desmond, quite the opposite of what she had intended. She ignored another leer, and turned back to her Kindle.

"I bet you're gagging for it!"

Frances decided to stand her ground but to not say anything more. She leaned sideways against the head of the sun lounger, closed her eyes, and waited for the next onslaught. She heard a grunting, the rustle of material, and was then aware that he had bent over her and was hissing in her ear.

"Come back to my cabin for a quickie. We can make sweet music together."

The obnoxious presence of the man and his proximity to her body tipped Frances over the edge. With one swift, fluid movement she opened her eyes and whacked her Kindle against his genitals for all she was worth, savouring his sharp intake of breath. As he fell to his knees, she heard other sunbathers clapping, and Martin's booming voice behind her.

"What the hell's going on?"

Frances grinned up at him.

"'Call me Des' here was getting just a little too personal for my liking."

Martin crouched down on a level with Desmond, and whispered something in his ear, after which the man stood up with difficulty and hobbled quickly away. Frances threw Desmond's towel off the sunbed next to her and patted the seat.

"What did you say to him?"

"Never you mind." Martin slumped down and closed his eyes. "All you can be certain of is that he definitely won't be bothering you again."

"Had a good trip this morning?" Frances turned off her Kindle and looked at him."

"Not really. The tequila tasting was okay, although Ethel threw up three times on the way back. I've also been bitten to buggery." He checked the back of his ankle. "But I did get you this."

He fished in his pocket and brought out a small red box. Frances took it from him and opened it.

"Oh."

"It's an eternity ring. It means you'll be stuck with me for eternity. Now there's a thought, isn't it?"

It certainly was, and Frances did not want to think too long and hard about it. She took the ring out of its casing and put it on the third finger of her right hand.

"It's lovely. Thanks."

"My pleasure." Martin smiled at her. "Hey, I'm trying. I'm really trying."

"Yep." Frances nodded. "You can say that again."

***

Passengers moved away as the engines started up and the ship moved off. Frances picked up her Kindle, aware that her husband was watching her from his sunbed. She sighed and looked at him.

"What?"

"Nothing." He shrugged. "I was just thinking to myself what a lucky guy I am. You're beautiful. No wonder that chap was after you."

"He was just chancing his luck." Frances chuckled. "He's probably trying it on with somebody else now."

"I love you, Fran. I'm so sorry about everything."

"Let's enjoy the holiday." Frances waved away any further response. "Just like Rhona said."

CHAPTER 26

He could not sleep again. Something about the look in her eyes as he had passed her the eternity ring had kept him awake for three successive nights. Now he stood alone on the top forward deck as dawn broke, watching the ship's progress along the muddy waters of the Mississippi river, guided by the light of a pilot boat. In an hour or so they would be docking at Julia Street Port, New Orleans in the height of Mardi Gras celebrations. Martin had no particular wish to join in the revelry, and did not look forward to leaving the ship and having to be on guard for pickpockets. His greatest desire was to stay in bed holding Frances close to him, and to feel that she was receiving some kind of pleasure from the experience.

He could have killed for a cigarette. Martin sighed as the silhouetted Shell Tower of The Big Easy appeared on the horizon. All around him passengers were waking up. Some were already jogging around the deck below, and others were heading to the Ocean View café for their first coffee of the day, still clad in dressing gowns. He yawned and thought he heard a police siren coming from somewhere in the far distance.

A young woman wearing a sweatshirt and shorts, and with her

blonde hair raked back into a ponytail came into view briefly as she turned the corner on the jogging track. Martin found himself waiting for her return. Looking over the railing he admired the woman's figure and noticed how she was not wearing any wedding ring. He laughed ruefully to himself; in the old days he would have made sure to jog along beside her and start up a conversation, but now the idea was anathema to him. Keeping Frances happy was his main concern, but his efforts were doing nothing to banish a growing anxiety that for all intents and purposes he was now flogging a dead horse.

He turned away from the railing and made his way down to the café, joining the queue for take-away hot beverages. After filling a polystyrene cup to the brim with milky tea just the way she liked it, he slapped on a lid and carried on down to deck seven. He could hear no TV blaring away in her cabin, and debated whether to ring her phone. The hands of his watch moved around to seven thirty, and heat fell away from the cup while he lay on his bed and waited. When he heard her flush the toilet he jumped up in eagerness and tapped lightly on the inter-connecting door.

"It's the tea boy. I've got you a cup, although it's getting a bit cold now."

The sound of a bolt being undone filled him with joy. She stood in the doorway still wearing pyjamas and with the ship's dressing gown tied tightly around her waist.

"You were up early." She took the cup from him, unsmiling. "Thanks."

"We're just about to dock in New Orleans. It's a great view up on top. I've been watching the last stretch down the Mississippi."

He thought she looked rather tired.

"The couple on the other side were partying until about three o'clock. I've slept in a bit later." Frances yawned. "I'm looking forward to my nice quiet bed back home."

He laughed.

"It's Mardi Gras time. Nobody sleeps here until the end of February. You could have come in here; you don't hear a peep out of the two next door to me."

"Well, I don't think so, do you?" She gave him a stare and took a sip of tea.

"The bed's big enough. I won't bite." He shrugged. "All that stuff's over with now."

He met her gaze and waited eagerly for a response.

"I'm going back for a shower. Thanks for the tea. Give me twenty minutes and then we can go up for some breakfast."

The tone of her voice instantly dashed his expectations. He turned away from the door, ran a hand through his hair, and wondered when on earth his wife was going to give him the benefit of the doubt.

***

He hadn't noticed it earlier, but somebody had draped gold, purple and green beads around the walls of the Ocean View Café. Crew members were handing out strings of plastic beads at the door as well as the usual hand sanitiser, and Martin stepped back in alarm.

"Men are wearing them too." Frances admonished. "Don't be a party pooper."

"What is it with these bloody beads? I feel a bit of a twat walking around with them." He grumbled. "It's just not me."

He liked her little trilling laugh.

"You booked the holiday, and now you've got to wear the beads."

Reluctantly he allowed her to drape two strings around his neck.

"Don't stick any photos of me wearing beads on Facebook."

Pleased that he had made her laugh, he followed her as she bagged a table.

"You guard our place, Beady, and I'll be back in a minute."

The café was heaving. He followed her with his eyes as she queued up for sausages, eggs and bacon. He came to the conclusion he would have stuck beads around his penis if that was all it took to make her come back to him.

CHAPTER 27

"They're coming from all directions. Someone's making a fortune knocking out boxes of frigging beads!"

He looked at the balcony above and reached up an arm, expertly catching a shower of beads before they had a chance to hit the floor.

"Bourbon Street is amazing!" Frances grinned and took the beads from him. "Did you think it'd be like this?"

"Not really." He kept an eye out for more raining beads. "I thought it'd be full of smoky little jazz clubs off the street that you have to climb downstairs into. It's a bit too touristy for me. Too many people."

He put an arm protectively around Frances' shoulders, and to his surprise she did not pull away.

"I wonder what it's like out of Mardi Gras season?" She looked up at him. "All the bars are heaving, and it's only eleven o'clock in the morning. Oh look, someone's put loads of beads around that statue of Fats Domino."

He followed behind Frances towards a bar where people sat outside in the sunshine listening to a rhythm and blues band. All around them were bronze statues of famous jazz musicians. He found the last two seats, ordered some beers, and watched his wife soaking up the atmosphere.

"This is better than rocking and rolling on a tender!"

She was in a happy mood, and he had no intention of bursting her bubble. However, he would have preferred it if she had picked somewhere a little less crowded.

"Don't forget we've got a tour around Saint Louis Cemetery Number One in an hour." He downed half a glass of beer in one go."It's where they filmed that bit in Easy Rider. When I phoned the tour guide he said the film company broke into the cemetery and filmed without permission."

"Really?" She looked at him with interest. "But trust you to remember *that* scene."

"Well…" He drained his glass with a grin. "I've looked at the map; it's not too far to walk."

***

The outer walls of the cemetery shielded the noise of the city, and the relative silence after Bourbon Street and the crumbling over-ground tombs held a strange fascination for him as he stood with Frances under the shade of a palm tree listening to their guide.

"Fancy that; the bodies are left to burn in the tombs by the heat of the sun and then a year or two later the ashes are swept into a hole at the back, and hey presto, there's room for another member of the family."

"It's a bit creepy." Frances made a face. "I preferred Bourbon Street."

Martin snapped away with his camera.

"We had to come today. It's not open tomorrow on Mardi Gras Day, and the ship sails the morning after. There's another forty five of these cemeteries all around the city, apparently the dead outnumber the living by ten to one."

"Not at Mardi Gras though." Frances chuckled.

She was thawing out. Martin smiled, stood back, and held the camera out to focus it.

"Stay under the tree. I want to take your picture."

"The group's moving off."

"We'll catch up in a minute."

She posed awkwardly as he clicked, eager to be away. She had picked up a slight tan in the preceding days, and he wanted to pick her up in his arms and never let her go.

"Here; have another row of beads. They're weighing me down."

He took off a purple string and placed it around her neck, pulling her towards him at the same time.

"You look lovely today, if you don't mind me saying so."

"I'm not Karen Black."

"And I'm not Peter Fonda, but hey, I *do* love you. You know that, don't you?"

"Yes I know." She nodded. "Come on, the tour's nearly over; let's find some lunch."

***

They made their way towards the Riverside Shopping Mall, where a blues quartet played on the quayside. Frances pointed to a shady spot.

"Let's sit down and listen awhile. There's plenty of time to buy presents."

"I'll get some burgers and chips from that stall over there." Martin nodded. "I'll be back in a minute."

"Is that all Americans eat?" Frances wondered aloud. "I haven't seen any vegetables yet, apart from on the ship. And fries- they're called fries. Chips seem to be crisps over here."

"I'll get two burgers and crisps then, and ask if they've got any broccoli on the side."

"Whatever." Frances lay back on the grass. "I'm knackered."

He enjoyed the companionable silence as they devoured their lunch. All around them people danced to the music, or wandered around various food outlets along the quayside. Martin wiped his mouth with the back of his hand.

"I'm really enjoying today. Are you pleased you came here now?" He watched her face for a reaction.

"Yeah, it's nice to have experienced it, but we've got to go on a street car before we go back to the ship as well. I overheard a conversation in the theatre last night. They mentioned street cars go up to the French market. What d'you think?"

"Sure, we can do that tomorrow before the carnival parade. After shopping for the next sixteen hours for presents to take home I think I'd have had enough for today."

"You always did exaggerate." She laughed. "I'm only going to buy them all tee shirts, otherwise our suitcases won't close."

They stood up, and he took her hand as they made their haphazard way through the crowds, noticing with a surge of relief that she did not pull it away.

CHAPTER 28

He could hear the phone ringing in her cabin as he held the receiver to his ear.

"I'm going to have a shower. What's up?"

Her tone of voice did not seem as strident as usual. Martin checked his watch.

"It's a formal night in the main dining room. Do you want to dress up, or shall we go to the café?"

"I've bought a posh frock. How about you?"

"Yeah, I've got one as well."

"A frock?"

"Yep, it goes well with my beads."

The sound of her laughter was music to his ears.

"Okay, let's do the main dining room tonight. I'll open the middle door when I'm ready."

He was smiling as he ended the call. Hanging up in his wardrobe was the white dinner jacket and bow tie that he'd hired the week before; he felt pleased that he'd now have a chance to wear it.

***

In his opinion he still scrubbed up pretty good for someone pushing sixty. Martin tweaked the bow tie into place and smoothed some gel into his hair; he could have done with his travel iron, but he remembered how the bastards had confiscated it on the day they'd arrived. He hoped she didn't notice the horizontal crease in his trousers, and if he kept the jacket on all night then he reasoned the shirt wouldn't look too bad.

He sat carefully on the end of the bed and flicked impatiently through the TV channels. When he heard the bolt being thrown back he jumped up and turned towards the inter-connecting door, his breath catching in his throat at the sight of her. The spotlight shining above them enhanced the new red highlights in her hair, and the long black chiffon Laura Ashley creation clung to her womanly figure in all the right places.

"You look lovely." He sighed. "I'm such a lucky guy."

Although she remained silent, he thought she appeared pleased at his compliment. He held her hand as they sauntered along the corridor and downstairs into the deck 4 dining room, just in time to grab the last table for two. He felt about ten feet tall, and wanted the evening to last forever.

Slight nervousness at voicing the thoughts in his head had caused him to make generous inroads into a bottle of house wine. He could see her watching every drop he drank, and there and then decided to do what he had never done before; he put a hand over the top of his glass when the waiter returned to take their order.

"No more thanks."

The waiter nodded politely, made a note of their order, and moved away to the next table. He could see Frances looking at him with undisguised amusement.

"I never thought I'd see the day!"

"It's the new me." He replied. "No longer the piss-head. All I want to do is to be what you want me to be."

"But that would make you miserable, and you'd eventually resent me." She shook her head. "You have to live true to yourself."

"Living true to myself nearly split us up for good." He stated firmly. "You've been right all along. I've been a total shit, living as a single bloke when I should have been considering you. No wonder you've had enough."

He looked out of the porthole to his left. The lights of Julia Street twinkled enticingly. Out in the city a million couples were getting it together, and he wanted to be one of them. Opposite, Frances was regarding him with her usual suspicion.

"I'm enjoying the holiday, but as soon as we get home the problem still remains that I cannot trust you or believe one word you say."

The soup arrived, and he took both of her hands in his before she had a chance to pick up a spoon.

"That was then, this is now. Give me another chance and I'll prove to you that I've changed."

"How many times have we had this conversation?" She rolled her eyes to the heavens. "I can't let you do this to me again!"

"We've got two sons and two lovely grandchildren. We're *family*. Families stick together through thick and thin. You know me inside out. I know you hate me leaving the toilet seat up. I can't stand you using my razor to shave your legs. But hey, little things like that we can get round. Help me sort out the big things."

"Like your penchant for prostitutes and porn? And how about what you get up to when you go away on business?" Frances gave a snort. "I've given up trying to sort *those* ones out. Where *do* you hide all the porn by the way?"

He let her pull away from his grasp. She laid a serviette on her lap, and lifted a spoonful of soup to her lips. He was desperate to break the silence.

"Under the floorboards in the front room; that's where I *hid* it, past tense. There's nothing there now of course, I've chucked it all out, but that's where it was."

"Huh, no wonder I could never find anything." She laughed ruefully. "I used to scour the house from top to bottom when you were out."

He swallowed some soup before his counter-attack.

"So how about you? Where did you hide that voice recorder then? What about *him*?"

She ate slowly, but looked uncomfortable at his remark.

"The first one belonged to the hospital, but when I left I bought a replacement and kept it under my bed. You found it in your van. There isn't another one. *He's* still with his wife and children I expect. He's not interested in me."

"Then he's a fool." His face registered relief as he put down his spoon and looked at her. "So we're even?"

Her audible sigh sent a shiver running through him.

"Martin, we can't go on like this, with neither of us trusting the other one. You're still worried in case I've bought another voice recorder, and God only knows what you're doing when you're not at home. You're so bloody *secretive*!"

"I still love you, Fran." He ignored the waiter collecting the empty soup plates. "Let's start again. What d'you say?"

Her retort dashed whatever hopes he had for the remainder of the evening. She dabbed at her lips with the serviette and gave him a steely stare.

"Haven't we already had this conversation? I say just let's enjoy this meal and the holiday, and stop going over old ground."

CHAPTER 29

She had second thoughts about climbing up the bleachers to the top, just as Martin found them a seat and stood looking up and down St. Charles Avenue.

"We'll get a good view from here. The Krewes of Orpheus and Proteus start at quarter past five and then six o'clock apparently."

Frances thought it best to voice her concerns. She sat down on the top step and tapped his leg.

"But we'll be trapped. At home there'd be aisles in the middle of the grandstands, but here there's nothing. Once more coachloads arrive we won't be able to get down again until the parade's over.

"Our coach doesn't go until quarter to ten. We'll be okay, unless you really want to sit down there at the bottom?"

"Yeah, I think I do." She nodded. "What if we're up here and need the loo?"

Martin stuck his legs out and crossed one tightly over the other.

"Hold it 'till we get back on the ship!"

"I don't think so." She stood up. "Come on, let's sit on the front row."

They climbed back down the bleachers and bagged two seats at the end of the first row in front of the guard rail.

"Happy now?" Martin turned towards her.

"Great." She nodded enthusiastically. "Thanks for that."

With the arrival of three more coach loads of cruise passengers, the bleachers were soon full. Frances looked in horror as elderly and infirm people attempted to climb up past them to a spare seat.

"God, I'm glad we moved." She shuddered slightly. "After the parades end, one of them has only got to fall trying to get back to ground level, and everyone will go down like a set of dominoes."

Just before the parade began another coach load of passengers arrived at the bleachers. On finding the seats all taken, they spread out along the front of the guard rail.

"Great." Martin complained bitterly. "Now we can't see a bloody thing. We should have stayed up the top." He tapped a guy standing in front of him. "Hey, we can't see anything now."

"Not my problem, mate." The reply came with a British accent. "We've paid the same money as you, and we haven't even got a seat. We've got nowhere else to go."

There were no spaces along the railings. Martin and Frances stood up just as the first brass band came into view and made its way down St. Charles Avenue. An irritable male voice came from behind Frances.

"Sit down!"

"Hey! Don't you shout at my wife to sit down!" Martin turned and prodded the complainant with one finger. "Stand up or shut the fuck up!"

"Martin, leave it." Frances shook her head. "It doesn't matter. I'll sit down."

The band's bass drum players were giving it their all, and trumpets sounded above the noise of shouting and cheering from the bleachers. Cheer-leaders danced in unison and fire-eaters twirled dangerous looking rods, the heat radiating towards where Frances sat. She heard Martin shout in her ear.

"Stand up, you'll see better!"

She felt him lifting her into a standing position, but then from behind came a strong push, temporarily knocking her to the ground. As she scrambled to her feet she was horrified to discover her husband had hurled himself onto the middle-aged man sitting above and behind her and was throwing punches to his face, scattering the crowds on either side, who began climbing down the bleachers to get away.

"Martin! Stop it!" Frances screamed over the noise of the brass band. "We'll be chucked out!"

She could tell he was taking out all the anger and frustration at his current situation on the stranger. The man, having landed a retaliatory punch, held up his hands in supplication as her husband gave him another prod.

"Nobody pushes my wife!"

"Sorry mate." The man rubbed his jaw. "These upper seats are too fucking dangerous to stand up in."

With relief she could see Martin, lip bleeding slightly and panting, wiping his mouth on his sleeve and turning back to the parade, just as a row of beads landed on his head from a passing float. Beside himself with fury, he threw them back in the direction of the astonished and masked Krewe member.

"Keep your fucking beads!"

People standing by the railings in front of them edged away, and Frances suddenly found that she had the best view of all.

***

"How's the lip?"

In the darkness of the coach she watched as he lay back against the headrest and closed his eyes.

"Fine; it's nothing."

"Thanks for sticking up for me though." She linked her arm in his. "I'll always think of tonight when I make pancakes in the future. I don't think that chap expected to get his beads back again so soon."

She watched a slow grin spread over his face and he gave her arm a squeeze.

"I've had a great night and a bloody good holiday. Thanks Fran."

"My pleasure, I think." She sighed. "I'm so sorry I can't give you what you want."

"Give us time." He leaned over and kissed her forehead. "We'll get there."

CHAPTER 30

She came to the conclusion there was nothing worse than jet-lag, sore eyes, and two suitcases full of dirty washing. Frances yawned and picked up the mountain of post lying on the mat as Martin locked up the car and followed in behind her, dropping his keys on the hall table.

"Back to work tomorrow. What about you, Fran?"

"I've got another day off and then an early shift on Tuesday."

She sifted through the post, handing over the letters not addressed to her. One, franked with the Sunset Care Home's mark, interested her more than the others. She filled up the kettle and switched it on whilst ripping open the envelope.

'Hi Fran,

Just a quick note. Our syndicate ticket won £750,000 on Euromillions last Friday. Your share is £150,000! Mavis is sorting the money out with the advisor, and it'll be paid into our accounts by bank transfer. It's a nice amount. Not enough to give up work, but as they say, a nice little earner. We only had your landline number by the way. See you Tuesday. All the best, Deana.'

She had to read it through three times before it began to sink in. The kettle came to the boil and she glanced at the note once more before folding it in quarters and sticking it down the front of her bra. Behind her Martin opened the fridge door.

"Just long life milk left. We'll have to go shopping later."

"Sure." She felt stupefied, as though on another planet. "Use that for now."

***

Tired beyond belief but unable to sleep, Frances flicked a switch to turn on the bedside lamp and felt under her pillow to take yet another look at Deana's note. There it was in black and white again, the fact that she would soon be £150,000 richer. It was as though fate had drawn her towards the care home and all the new friends she had made there in such a short space of time. In her hands now lay the means to branch out and forge a new life of her own; free from mistrust, suspicion, and lies. No longer would she need to wonder what her husband was up to; she could forget him and leave him to stew in the morass of his own making.

She plumped up the pillow and sunk her head down in its feathery depths willing sleep to rest a mind spinning into overdrive. She could not shift the mental image of her own little rented flat within walking distance of the care home, *and* with her own TV remote. She would have total control over all her possessions, and would never again need to turn out boxes and search through the house looking for any secrets that Martin was trying to hide.

She gave herself a little hug of glee, but knew that she must bide her time and wait until the money was safely in her account before doing the rounds of estate agents in the town centre to find her dream property. She could put down six months' rent in advance, and still be able to pay the bills and buy food from her wages. Things were looking up. Somewhere, just out of sight, she was sure an angel was watching over her.

***

Two weeks later her bank account had swelled beyond all recognition. Frances gave Mavis a hug on entering the staff room early the following morning, and then grabbed a tardy Sylvia. The three of them jumped up and down in a huddle.

"I can't believe it!"

"It's true! What're you going to do with it Fran?"

"Something I should have done years ago but never had the money to do it with."

"Oh?" Mavis looked at her with interest.

"I'm going to move into my own little flat. I can't bloody well wait."

"You're leaving the wonderful Martin?"

"Actually he's not so wonderful." Frances grimaced. "Sylvia, you're welcome to him."

"All men are pervs." Sylvia hooted. "It's that willy, it does their heads in."

"Me and Pete are going to Montego Bay for a belated silver wedding anniversary, and then will pay off some of our son's mortgage." Mavis broke free and hung up her coat. "I'm still coming back to work afterwards though."

"I'm going to have another bedroom and bathroom built on the back of my house and take in a lodger." Sylvia put on her overall. "Who knows, I might get a hunk who wants to stay there and pay me some rent."

"Good luck with that." Frances smiled at Sylvia. "Although if I can't find a flat it might be me."

Sylvia raised a thumb towards Frances.

"Your old man doesn't know what he's got coming."

"Oh well." Frances shrugged. "He'll find out soon enough."

As she locked her coat and bag away she tried to picture her husband's face on reading the note that she should have written many, many years before.

CHAPTER 31

MARTIN

After a few days away on business he now looked forward to coming home a lot more than he had done in the past. Usually she would have rooted out anything he had been careless enough to leave out, and consequently he would be in the doghouse for at least a fortnight. Now he knew there was nothing for her to find. She had been quieter than usual of late, but at least they were not arguing anymore.

Martin pulled up on the driveway and then reversed a little bit more towards the house to give Frances room to park after her shift ended. He stretched as he opened the driver's door and got out of the van. It had been a long drive back from Newcastle, and he needed a hot shower.

The hallway smelt of pot pourri as he turned his key in the lock. He wondered if she had left him a nice plate of something to heat up, and decided to check the fridge before going upstairs.

The fluorescent light spluttered into life, and he looked around the kitchen with satisfaction. His wife had left everything orderly, just as he liked it. Martin pulled open the fridge door and smiled on seeing a dinner plate on the top shelf covered with a microwave lid. He glanced at it a second time. On top of the microwave lid was an envelope, but he decided to read its contents after a wash. He grabbed a pint of milk before closing the fridge door, and guzzled the first quarter straight from the bottle before leaving it out on the draining board.

New fluffy towels were warming up in the bathroom on the heated rail. Martin threw off his clothes, just missing the laundry basket, and padded over to the shower, enjoying the pummelling of hot water on his skin. Dried, powdered, and dressed in clean jeans and a jumper, he found his slippers on the upstairs landing and decided to have a little peep around the closed door of his wife's bedroom before she returned from work. He loved the smell of her perfume, which always seemed to hang on the air.

Whistling a little tune, he turned the handle but then stepped back in amazement. Even by the light of the landing he could see that not one trace of his wife remained. Her bed had gone, together with her dressing gown and two wardrobes. All that was left was a low voltage bulb hanging from the ceiling. He blinked and switched on the bedroom light to confirm what he had just seen. He had been correct; the room was empty.

Running downstairs like a madman, Martin threw the fridge door wide and ripped open the envelope on top of his dinner, pulling out a sheet of his wife's now familiar rose-scented notepaper.

'Dear Martin,

I'm sorry it has to be this way, but I know that if you'd been home you would never have let me leave. I have my own flat now. I just cannot carry on living with somebody I do not trust. You've been a great father, but as far as I'm concerned have fallen terribly short in the husband department.

The Euromillions syndicate at work won £750,000, and my share was enough to rent a flat, buy some new furniture, and have a nice little bit of money left over. Colin and Richard helped me to move, although I didn't tell them why I was leaving and they didn't ask. I cooked myself a casserole last night in my new flat, and popped over today to leave you some and also this note. I took my bedroom furniture and the slow cooker (because you've never used it), but the rest of the stuff in the house is yours.

I must live true to myself, and can no longer be the porn detective that I became when living with you. I've had enough. I hope you find somebody to fulfil your needs, because God knows I cannot. Perhaps in time you will come to understand my point of view, but for now I know that you are angrier with me than you have ever been.

Obviously we will still have to meet at family functions and so I hope that one day we can be friends, but until that day please let me live my life in peace. Yours, Frances.'

***

He was not sure how long he had stayed there looking at the note. Martin, his appetite gone, sat at the table where he and his wife and sons had long ago loved and laughed together before his porn addiction, secretiveness and infidelity had ruined their marriage. Now he realised he could look at as much porn as he wanted to, but the irony of the situation was that he never wanted to see another pair of tits again for the rest of his whole, miserable life. He tried to ring her mobile phone; it was dead.

CHAPTER 32

"Martin! It's lovely to see you again!" Rhona opened the front door wide. "Do come in. Is Frances with you?"

"That's what I want to talk to you about." Martin shook his head.

"Carry on through. You know where to go."

It seemed strange sitting on the two-seater settee without his wife. Martin looked around him nervously as Rhona made herself comfortable and leafed through a notepad.

"Did the two of you manage to get away?"

"We had a nice cruise, yes. We were in New Orleans for the Mardi Gras."

"Wonderful!" Rhona smiled. "How did it go?"

"I thought we were getting on very well, but then Frances had a win on Euromillions and moved out." Martin took a piece of paper out of his pocket. "I had this *Dear John* letter."

"Ah." Rhona skimmed briefly through the note. "I see."

"What do you suggest I do now?" Martin shrugged. "I'm at a loss."

He was conscious of Rhona's eyes on him, and he looked away.

"Have you managed to talk to your wife?"

"She's switched off her phone." Martin shook his head. "It's hopeless. I don't even know where she's staying."

Rhona leaned forward in her chair.

"If you want your wife back, you must fight for her. You had a good holiday by the sound of it, and therefore both of you will have some good memories to work with. I'm sure you know where she can be found, even if you don't know where she is living. Make her see you're serious about wanting her back. Don't give up."

***

He'd had to put a customer off, but it was worth it just to be able to speak to his wife. Martin sat in his van in a side street opposite the Sunset Care Home the following day, and waited for Frances to appear. Around 2.30pm he was rewarded by the sight of her familiar figure turning left out of the home, and heading for the high street.

He quickly locked his van and crossed the road, gaining speed in order to decrease the distance between them. At the end of the high street he noticed her turning left into Jade Gardens, a street consisting mainly of large Victorian houses with a selection of doorbells on the front porches.

Martin slowed his pace as Frances stopped to rummage through her bag before opening a gate and walking up the path to number 12. With no time to waste, he caught the gate before it closed and ran along behind her.

"Sorry I had to do this, but I couldn't get you on the phone."

She whipped her head around at the sound of his voice. Her features gave nothing away.

"I was waiting for something like this." She shrugged. "But I was hoping you might have calmed down first."

"I am calm." He kept his voice even. "I can promise you that you won't need to call the police."

He heard her give an audible sigh.

"You'd better come in then."

The hallway emitted an aroma of stale cabbage. Martin wrinkled his nose and followed behind Frances as she climbed a flight of stairs to a first floor flat.

"Nice neighbours?" He looked around and noticed stairs going up to a third floor.

"They're okay. Malcolm, a young chap below, and Emma, a nurse, lives at the top."

"No wild parties then?"

"Not yet." She kept her back to him. "Give me time though."

He watched her as she struggled to turn a key in the lock.

"I can help fix that if the lock's a bit stiff. I've got some lubricant in the van."

"Yeah, I bet you have."

He could have bitten his tongue out. Martin let the innuendo slide and keeping a respectable distance, followed his wife down a short hallway to the living room. He moved in the direction of her pointing finger.

"You have the armchair. I'll sit on the settee."

He sat down on a soft pale green leather armchair.

"The boys must have had a struggle getting these up the stairs."

"I paid them well, and they were happy to do it." She took off her coat. "Coffee?"

"Ta." He nodded. "Something smells nice."

"It's my casserole in the slow cooker."

His mouth began to salivate; he was starving. Martin swallowed hard and looked around the room when Frances disappeared off to the kitchen. All the furniture appeared new and solid. The cream shag-pile carpet looked expensive. He was impressed.

He wondered what was steaming in the bowls when she returned carrying a tray.

"I couldn't eat my lunch while you sit there with nothing, so make the most of it."

The casserole was delicious and the coffee hot and sweet; she knew just how he liked it. Martin sat back in the armchair, replete.

"That was lovely. Let me do something to repay you. Have you got any jobs that need doing?"

"Well, there is one thing." Frances sipped her coffee. "The TV isn't working properly. There's an aerial in the loft apparently, but I can't get up there and even if I could, I wouldn't know the correct way to attach any cables."

Martin felt buoyed up at the thought.

"I'll bring my long ladder tomorrow and do it for you."

"Cheers. I'll cook you something if you like?"

"There's no need." He shook his head. "I'm happy to do it."

"No, I like to pay my way, so to speak. I'll do some fish and chips. I've got a late shift tomorrow."

"Only if you're sure." He could not believe his luck, and stuck his neck out a little bit more. "It's a shame you've moved out. I thought we were getting on so well on holiday."

She shrugged.

"We were, but there's the age-old problem that I don't trust you and probably never will do. I came to the conclusion that the only way I could get around that was to move out and stop worrying all the time about what you were getting up to when I wasn't around."

"All that shit has stopped now." He let out a sigh. "I keep telling you that."

"Let me put it this way." He thought Frances put her cup down a little too forcefully on the coffee table. "If you were me, would *you* believe anything you were saying?"

Martin gave a rueful laugh and raised the palms of both hands.

"Look, I know I've lied to you in the past, but there comes a time when you've just got to start giving me the benefit of the doubt."

"Easier said than done." Frances leaned back in her seat. "I'm so guarded now about not getting let down again by you, that I just cannot believe a single word you say."

"Well, believe *this*." Martin sat forward and looked at her. "I *will* be here after your late shift tomorrow and fix your TV. That's a start, right?"

He was relieved to see a small nod from his wife.

"Right." Frances affirmed. "I'm sure you will be."

He knew that nothing, neither hell, fire, brimstone nor flood, would stop him knocking on her front door the next day.

CHAPTER 33

He tried to ignore Malcolm, whose neck was craning out of a bathroom window. Martin, perched on a ladder, carried on fixing cable clips to a new aerial wire running up the outside wall of Frances' flat towards the soffits.

"What're you doin'?"

Martin took a clip out of his mouth and gave the young guy a stare.

"Peeling spuds, mate."

"You need permission for that."

"To peel spuds?" Martin hammered in another clip. "Frances said yes."

"No, not from Fran." Malcolm's returned the glare. "From the landlord."

"Bollocks to the landlord." Martin shrugged. "I'm saving him money anyway."

He pushed the end of the wire through into the roof space and started down the ladder, giving a wide grin in the direction of the bathroom window.

"You're an arrogant bastard aren't you?"

"Look, I've got enough grief in my life without you starting as well." Martin raised his middle finger. "Why don't you just go inside and boil your bits somewhere?"

The bathroom window slammed shut, and Martin wondered whether there was anybody in the vicinity who actually did *not* want to give him a rollicking.

***

"Thanks, that's a great picture now."

He finished up the last piece of haddock, pleased with his wife's expression.

"Your landlord's a bit of a bodger. I'll replace that ceiling rose in your bathroom tomorrow. There's a bad connection in the loft, and the wiring's a bit hot."

"Oh goodness." Frances picked up the remote control and switched off the TV. "Perhaps I'd better tell him."

"Nah, he'll get the tit ache once he knows I've been fiddling about up there. At least it'll put my own mind at rest though."

He heard her exhale, but whether it was a sigh of irritation at putting up with his presence for yet another evening, or whether it was due to the landlord's incompetence he had not the foggiest idea.

"Well, if you don't mind then…"

As her words petered out he knew he was onto a winner.

"No probs. Another late shift tomorrow?"

"Yes, I'll be home about seven thirty."

"Then I'll be on your doorstep at seven thirty one."

She gave him a feeble smile.

"Yes, I know you will. It'll be liver and bacon casserole tomorrow."

He smacked his lips.

"My favourite."

***

He refrained from asking for a second helping, and waggled his fork in the direction of the TV.

"Even Channel five's got a good picture."

He watched her wiping a last piece of bread around the plate.

"Malcolm says the picture on his TV isn't as good as mine, even after the landlord supposedly mended it."

Martin fixed his wife with a questioning glance.

"Has he been up here then?"

"Yeah." Frances nodded. "After you went, he came up to have a look. He said he'll pay you to do his as well."

"Bloody cheek! Let him do his own! He called me an arrogant bastard."

He caught his wife's grin just before it disappeared.

"Well, you *can* be a bit short sometimes, let's face it. He didn't know you were my husband."

Martin rolled his eyes to the heavens.

"Oh, so now the whole street knows our business then?"

"No." Frances shook her head. "Just Malcolm, and he's very discreet."

He realised the possible advantage just in time.

"Alright. Will you be here at the weekend?"

He was relieved to see a small nod.

"Mostly. It's my weekend off."

"Tell him I'll come round on Saturday afternoon then."

"Okay, but now I want a long soak in the bath and an early night."

He sensed his presence was no longer required, and stood up.

"See you on Saturday."

"Okay."

CHAPTER 34

FRANCES

She could not get out of the habit of buying enough food for two people. Frances sat down at the kitchen table after her Friday late shift, looked at the huge plateful of fare before her, and expanded the belt of her trousers by one notch. As she bit into a roast potato she decided to invite Malcolm and Emma to dinner more often, otherwise the only other option would be to start buying bigger clothes.

The weekend stretched before her. Bernie had suggested that she might like to help him with the homeless Saturday evening soup and sandwich rota, to which she had readily agreed. She liked Bernie's quiet, calm manner, and the gentle way he spoke to the care home residents. She chewed thoughtfully and considered how the years of looking after an elderly mother might have given him a compassion not usually seen in members of the male sex. The Euromillions win had not changed him one iota; he still presented for work every day, and to her knowledge had not even thought of updating his five year old Ford Focus.

Frances speared a piece of chicken with a fork and gave a little grin to herself. The train journey up to London with Bernie would ensure she was not around when Martin turned up with another aerial lead. Her husband was becoming a little too keen to do any odd jobs; in the past she had previously needed to ask him at least three or four times to do something, whereby he would have told her to stop nagging, and not carried out the task until it had suited him. As far as she was concerned, his current eagerness to comply with her wishes could only mean one thing.

***

She had not been to Charing Cross station for years. Frances looked around her; the station was still recognisable from the New Year's Eves of her youth, although now somewhat larger and noisier. Nameless people rushed to and fro, making her feel small and rather insignificant. She followed behind Bernie, as he made his way out into the Strand.

"It's just across the road by St. Martin-in-the-Field church. It's not a bad crowd on a Saturday night. You get the odd mouthy one who's had too much to drink, but on the whole they're all grateful for something to eat."

Volunteers were already setting up as they arrived, with tureens of soup being carried out into the street from the church to rest on long tables. A couple of volunteers waved at Bernie, who made the introductions. Frances smiled at her new friends, and looked wistfully across at the view of Trafalgar Square as she and Bernie unpacked plastic containers of sandwiches and fruit cake from sealed cardboard boxes.

"Last time I was up here I think I must have been about eighteen or nineteen."

"Did you jump in the fountains?" Bernie chuckled. "They rope them all off on New Year's Eve now."

"I did once, yes." Frances nodded. "I had to go home soaked

through and freezing cold. All my own fault, as my mother reminded me at the time."

"We've all been young and silly. I used to come up here with a group of mates. We used to wolf down our Wimpys and then run as fast as we could along Shaftesbury Avenue and hope we weren't being chased for payment."

"Really?" Frances laughed. "I can't imagine you doing that."

"I confess right now." Bernie's eyes twinkled merrily. "Er…do you want to do the soup or the sandwiches? It's a case of making sure everybody gets something and not letting others slope off with bags of goodies they're not entitled to."

"I don't mind." Frances shrugged. "It's just nice to do something different."

"Yeah, if you ladle the soup out into those bowls, then we can make a start in a minute."

She could only feel grateful for her new little flat and warm bed as a long line of homeless people began to shuffle along in front of her. After a while her right arm began to ache from lifting the ladle and she switched to her left, causing a few more spills on the Formica-covered tables. Other volunteers kept the tureens full, and Frances considered that she hadn't enjoyed a Saturday night so much for years. She felt needed instead of worthless, and was quite disappointed when the last tureen of soup was empty.

"Thanks for inviting me, Bernie." Frances shook his hand in gratitude. "I can see why you like coming here."

"I love it." Bernie clasped one huge hand over her own. "Do come again, you're an expert ladler."

"My arms ache, it shows how unfit I am." Frances laughed. "Yes, I'd love to have another go."

***

She waved goodbye to Bernie at Ipswich station and walked swiftly back to her car. The evening had gone better than she could have ever hoped, and as she turned into Jade Gardens she was even humming a little tune to herself.

Underneath the street lamp outside number 16 was parked an all-too-familiar van. Frances watched the occupant sit up straighter in his seat at the sight of her and then jump out of the van, leaving the door open. She had barely enough time to switch the engine off before he had yanked open her driver's door.

"Where have you been all evening?"

She could tell by the tone of his voice that he was barely holding it all together. Frances climbed out of the driver's seat carefully, and used the open car door as a shield between them.

"Out with a friend."

"What friend? Where?"

She held one hand out, palm outstretched, across the door towards him.

"Martin, stop right there! I have a perfect right to go out with whom I please. We no longer live in the same house!"

Her voice rose in irritation. She swallowed hard and watched his expression as it abruptly changed from anger to sadness.

"I fixed your neighbour's aerial. I thought you'd be in this evening."

"I said I'd mostly be here during the weekend, but not all the time. Thanks for helping Malcolm out though."

"I did it for you." His voice sounded petulant. "Because you asked me to."

She stood in the street as the eleven o'clock church bell sounded and just for a moment wished for time to transport them back again to the happy couple they had once been before pornography had torn them apart. However, she realised that she had been deceived from the very beginning. Martin was not the man she thought she had married, and she had wasted over 30 years of her life playing porn detective and fretting about who her husband was having sex with on the side. She was stronger now; independent. She was in charge of her own future.

"I'm going to lock the car and go up to bed." She closed the car door gently. "Goodnight Martin."

CHAPTER 35

MARTIN

He had lost her through his own stupidity. Cheeky, bright Frances, with her optimistic views on life balancing his own tendency towards pessimism. They had been a good team. Now it was as though he had been cast adrift in life's turbulent seas without any safety raft.

Martin watched his wife walk up the path of number 12 Jade Gardens without even so much as a glance back in his direction. For the first time he felt a kind of futile impotence. Frances had found somebody else, and there was nothing whatsoever that he could do about it. He was glad nobody was around in the deserted street to witness him wiping his eyes.

What to do next? His mother had always told him to go out and get what he wanted, and he had wanted Frances from the very first moment he saw her.

The light went on in the middle flat, and he saw her pulling curtains across the bay window in the living room. Martin sank deeper into the driver's seat and remembered the first heady years of their marriage, before even Colin had been born, before porn had invaded their private world like a cancer. Now it seemed there was no remedy for their broken marriage. He let out a sob, punched the steering wheel, closed his eyes, and cursed his addictive nature to hell and beyond.

***

The tapping seemed to be coming from far away. He woke up with a start and for a split second had no idea where he was. When he looked to his left, he saw her rapping on the van's window and holding something steaming in a cup.

"Have you been here all night?"

The sight of his wife's concerned features brought him back to full consciousness. He opened the passenger door, took the proffered cup, and yawned.

"God, I must have dozed off. Next thing I knew you were knocking on the window."

"I opened the curtains and saw your van still here. I thought you'd want some coffee?"

"Lovely, ta." He took a sip. "Some Saturday night out *that* was."

"Were you supposed to be somewhere then?"

He laughed ruefully at her remark, and took another slurp of coffee.

"Yeah, out with *you* for dinner, but it seems you were otherwise occupied."

He saw a brief flash of irritation pass over her face.

"We hadn't made any plans, Martin. I helped out at a homeless shelter in London last night."

"Who with?"

"A friend from the home. And no, he's not my boyfriend; just a friend."

A wave of jealousy washed over him.

"How are we ever going to get back together if you're out every evening with another bloke?"

He knew he'd blown it as he watched her move away from the window.

"You need to go home and have a shower and some breakfast."

"I haven't been there to switch the hot water on. Can I have a wash at yours and a slice of toast?"

He could see her resolve crumbling as she wrestled with her conscience.

"Oh, okay then. Just don't make a habit of it."

"No, of course not." He jumped out of the van quickly before she had a chance to change her mind. "Cheers, Fran."

***

The smell of fried bacon made his mouth water as he climbed the stairs behind her.

"That's Malcolm's breakfast by the way, not mine. I had All Bran."

"I'm knocking on *his* door then. You know the effect bran has on me."

He looked up as she turned around to face him.

"How could I forget that trip to Scotland?" She rolled her eyes. "I think we must have stopped at every service station on the M6."

"It was the only thing left in the cupboard to eat." He shrugged. "Poor old Colin came off worse."

He could see she was grinning as they entered the flat.

"There's a clean towel in there, help yourself." She opened a cupboard in the hallway. "I seem to be seeing more of you now we're separated than I ever did when we lived in the same house."

"I was a bastard then." He stared into her clear grey eyes. "I'm so sorry, Fran."

"Enjoy your shower." She looked away and closed the cupboard. "There's beans on toast if you like when you come out."

"Lovely."

The hot cascading water eased the ache in his lower back. Martin towelled himself dry and looked around the bathroom, trying to guess whether the décor suggested 1950's or later. A spreading mould sent black tendrils over the ceiling above the shower, paint peeled from the skirting boards, and the old enamel bath had lost its plug. He wondered what time the local DIY shop opened. He shook his head and sighed at his wife's stubbornness.

CHAPTER 36

FRANCES

She looked up and admired the freshly-painted lemon coloured ceiling. The mould had not really bothered her, but now she could see just what a difference he had made to the bathroom in only one weekend. Matching pale yellow skirting boards complimented darker saffron and white tiling above the sink and bath, both of which had new plugs and chains and had been divested of their decades-old ring of grime around the middle. Frances finished up the last of the white emulsion and stepped back to admire her handiwork.

"The walls don't look half bad, do they? It's the first time I've ever done anything like this."

She looked towards Martin, perched on a ladder wrestling with a new light fitting.

"It now *looks* like a bathroom, instead of something out of a horror movie."

She made a face at him.

"It wasn't *that* bad!"

"Your landlord needs reporting, or shooting."

"I've only ever seen him once." Frances replied. "When I gave him my bank details."

"Yeah, I bet he wrote those down sharpish."

Frances stood her brush in a bucket of water and waited for the inevitable effect that the next words would have on him.

"I'm meeting Bernie in a while for another evening at the shelter."

His silence was unusual as she watched him screwing in the last of the spotlights. When he had finished he looked towards her with a shrug.

"I'm surplus to requirements then. I'll get home now."

She hid her surprise and smiled.

"Thanks so much for what you've done here."

"Any time." He climbed down the ladder and picked up his tool box. "You know where I am if you need me."

She peeped through the net curtains as he walked down the path towards his van. Frances, somewhat bemused at her husband's calm acceptance of her plans for the evening, noticed an air of resignation in his sagging shoulders. She wondered if he would return home or drive down to the red light district but then reminded herself that whatever he decided, he was now free to do as he wished. A pang of guilt crossed her features at the amount of work he had carried out at her flat, assuaged only by the knowledge he had done so of his own choosing. Shaking her head, Frances walked away from the window as Martin's van picked up speed along Jade Gardens.

***

Mindful of the fact that Bernie and tardiness did not go together, Frances parked her car at Ipswich station and waved to the now familiar figure waiting just inside the door as she ran towards him.

"Am I late?" She panted. "I've been a bit busy today."

"Nearly, I think the train for Liverpool Street arrives in about ten minutes."

She could feel his irritation. Frances carried on walking past

Bernie and onto the platform, knowing that Martin would more often than not have run hell for leather to the station at the last moment and caught the train by the skin of his teeth.

"We'd better not waste any more time then. It's going to take at least half a minute to walk to where we need to be."

"No need for sarcasm." Bernie followed on behind her. "It doesn't become you, Frances."

She stopped where she was and turned around to face him.

"Well, if we've still got another ten minutes, then I'm *not* late am I?"

"No, no, of course not. Let's just forget it, shall we?" Bernie's tone was calm and conciliatory, and he held out a packet boiled sweets. "Want one?"

"No thanks." Frances shook her head. "They make my teeth ache."

It was difficult for Frances to ignore the general slurping noises emanating from her travelling companion's mouth as they waited for the train, which arrived with every seat taken a quarter of an hour late. Forced to stand on a rocking train, she was tired before they had even arrived. When Bernie jumped into the only available seat at Newbury Park, Frances wondered if the evening could possibly get any worse. She came to the conclusion that although Martin had always had his brains in his pants, at least he would have offered her a chance to sit down. She was beginning to realise why Bernie had so far never found that elusive Miss Right.

CHAPTER 37

"I've asked Lucy to marry me, Mum."

Frances' mouth opened into a round 'o' of surprise.

"Really?" She smiled at Richard. "What did she say?"

"Er…the answer was *yes*. It seems she wants to be stuck with me for life."

Frances jumped up from the settee and gave her youngest son a hug.

"Well, she can do a lot worse. She's getting a fine young man."

Frances laughed as Richard put his cup down and stood up, enveloped her in a bear hug, and swung her around a couple of times before putting her gently down again on the carpet.

"I just wanted to make sure you're okay with it. I've told Dad. He shook my hand and gave me a beer."

"That sounds about right." Frances nodded and sat down next to her son. "Beer is his answer for most things."

"Don't be too hard on him." Richard admonished gently. "He's changed since he's been on his own. He's sad. I don't think he's drinking much at all now. I *know* he wants you back, Mum."

Frances sighed and took Richard's hand in hers.

"Rich, I'm happy here. I've got a job, and I'm getting on okay. It's not just the drink. There's things you don't know about. I just can't go back to him, believe me."

She noticed his hesitation before Richard spoke again

"Mum…will the two of you be okay at the wedding?"

Frances laughed.

"We won't be fighting hammer and tongs! Don't worry, I'll be civility personified, although I can't say the same for your father."

She thought she saw a frisson of relief pass over her son's features.

"Lucy and I would like to take you out to dinner tomorrow evening to celebrate. Is that okay?"

"Of course!" Frances nodded. "I'm on an early shift, so any time after five o'clock is great."

"We can meet up around six thirty; I'll text you the name of the restaurant when we've made up our minds." Richard stood up. "Thanks for the tea. By the way, Lucy's already booked Saint Mary's church for October the seventh."

"Wow." Frances smiled. "I'd better start thinking about a hat."

***

Her heart sunk when she saw the extra guest already seated at the table.

"You didn't tell me Dad was coming." Frances hissed in Richard's ear. "I bet he's already had three whiskies."

"We couldn't leave him out. "Lucy smiled at her. "He wanted to join in the celebration as well."

She walked in front of Richard and Lucy towards the table, as Martin stood up to greet them.

"Good news Fran, eh?" He kissed her cheek and then gave the happy couple a hug. "Who'd have thought old Rich would finally tie the knot?"

"Well, I suppose he had to sometime." She noticed with surprise a half empty bottle of mineral water in front of Martin's place. "Rich didn't say you were coming."

She saw Martin give his usual shrug.

"He didn't say *you* were coming either. He said he wanted to take me out to celebrate."

"Seems as though we've both been hoodwinked." Frances gave Richard a stare. "Never mind, let's sit down and have a look at the menu."

"They do lovely fish dishes here." Lucy piped up rather too eagerly as she took her seat. "I recommend the sea bass."

"Done." Martin laid down his menu. "What about you, Fran?"

Frances put on her reading glasses and scanned the menu.

"No, I think I'll have the beef stroganoff."

After the waiter had brought their drinks' orders she decided not to comment on her husband's choice of iced mineral water. Frances lifted her glass of Buck's Fizz.

"Here's to the bride and groom."

"Yeah." Martin clinked his glass with hers. "May all your troubles be little ones!"

"Steady on Dad." Richard laughed. "We don't want those for a few years yet."

"And here's to my new in-laws." Lucy clinked her glass of wine. "Thanks for coming out tonight."

"No problem." Frances smiled at Lucy. "I'll check with you what the colour scheme's going to be."

"Pink." Richard replied quickly. "Dad, you'll be wearing a pink suit and a pink cravat."

"Up yours." Martin laughed.

***

The evening had turned out better than she had hoped. Frances stood outside the restaurant and kissed Richard and then Lucy.

"Thanks for inviting me. I'll see you both soon. Congratulations again."

"I've had a great time." Lucy gave Frances a hug. "Have you got your car?"

"No, I walked." Frances replied. "It's not far from here to my flat."

"We'll give you a lift back if you like?"

"I'll do it, Lucy." Martin jangled his car keys. "Come on Fran, you don't want to walk about this time of night."

"I'm not some maiden in distress." Frances shook her head. "It's only a ten minute walk."

She saw the all-too-familiar stubborn look on her husband's face.

"Well, you can walk if you like, but I'll be kerb-crawling right behind you."

She could not be bothered to try and win the argument. With a final wave to Richard and Lucy, Frances walked to the kerbside, surprised as Martin stepped in front of her to open up the passenger door.

"You've never done this before. Am I wearing a crown or something?"

"It's the new me." Martin chuckled. "Get used to it."

She sank into the cream leather seat.

"You can get arrested for kerb crawling round here, although you've probably found that out."

She could not resist the pithy remark. The engine started and Martin made a U-turn along the high street towards Jade Gardens.

"I'm not even going to take the bait. I told you, I'm a changed man."

"If you say so." Frances replied, unconvinced.

"Give me time, and I'll prove it."

The car turned into Jade Gardens and came to a halt in the first available space.

"You've had thirty five years so far."

She did not resist as he switched off the engine and lifted one of her hands to his lips.

"I'm talking about the next thirty five. I've stopped drinking as well. I want to be that man you married."

"I don't want you to stop drinking." Frances sighed. "I want you to do just what you *want* to do. You're a free man now."

"It's what I want to do." He shrugged. "Someday I want you to come home, even if it does take another thirty five years."

"Jeez!" Frances laughed, removed her hand from his, and opened the door. "We'll be ninety years old!"

She stepped out of the car, gave him a wave, and walked up the path. As far as she was concerned, she *was* home. Martin would have to get used to it.

CHAPTER 38

She felt herself becoming attached to Elsie Jones. The elderly lady still had frequent bouts of lucidity, and that morning at the beginning of July Frances could tell it was going to be one of the 90 year old's better days. She steadied the frail body against a Zimmer frame as they headed in the general direction of the TV lounge. Frances followed a bony finger as it pointed towards her hand, while a reed-thin voice whispered in her ear.

"Didn't you used to wear a wedding ring?"

"Yes." Frances smiled. "But my husband and I are separated now."

She looked on with mild amusement as the old lady shook her head.

"I've been a widow for ten years, and it hasn't been much fun. Don't end up on your own. Make up and don't break up, that's what I say."

"I don't trust him." Frances replied gently. "Did you trust *your* husband?"

"About as far as I could throw him." The old lady cackled. "It's the companionship I missed when he died. He was always good to me and the children, but I knew he had another life that didn't include me. I turned a blind eye to it."

"I can't do that." Frances sighed. "I'd rather live on my own."

She stopped to allow Elsie to catch her breath.

"Bill would go off every now and again when he was younger, and do whatever with whoever." Elsie panted. "But he always came home to me. When he returned he was happy and loving. The children adored him. We never had a cross word in fifty six years of marriage."

"So you're saying ignore it if he has a mistress?" Frances looked at the old lady in puzzlement.

They reached the lounge and Elsie flopped down onto a chair.

"Life is hard, especially for women. It's still a man's world whatever they say. They earn more, and they have the advantage of a physical strength that we'll never have. Do *you* want to unblock drains?" Elsie cackled again. "Bill did all those horrible jobs, but sometimes a wife, especially one with a clutch of kids to look after, isn't enough for a man if you catch my drift."

Frances nodded as the old lady continued.

"Bill often had a fishing weekend away. I knew full well he wasn't going fishing, but it suited both of us to pretend he was."

"I'll bring you a cup of tea, Elsie." Frances smiled at the old lady. "I can't see me taking your advice, but thanks anyway."

Elsie Jones nodded and closed her eyes.

***

She looked around her living room at the furniture she had bought with her own money. In front of her on a tray was a dinner for one. Frances was alone, but she did not feel lonely. If she switched off the sound on her TV she could hear Malcolm watching the same channel downstairs. Emma often dropped in for a chat if their shifts allowed. She smiled and thought back to Elsie Jones' advice. Elsie had had 4 children to raise; no wonder she decided to turn a blind eye to Bill's philandering ways. Frances made herself a fish finger sandwich and mused on the joys of eating nursery food without having to cook a three course meal for a working man and two hungry sons.

She squirted more tomato sauce on the sandwich, and came to the conclusion that she was enjoying herself. Martin and the boys popped around every so often, but she thought her husband quite recently seemed more resigned to the single life. No longer did she worry about whether or not he had a mistress, in fact she hoped he *had* found somebody to share his life with. She realised as she filled her mouth with an exquisite flavour of fish finger that she had no desire whatsoever to return to the marital home and resume playing reluctant porn detective.

Did she need a man to feel fulfilled? Frances thought of Brian slurping boiled sweets and Martin's sexual peccadilloes. *Was there a man left upon this earth who did not fall short in some department? Did she really need a man to unblock the drains?* She came to the conclusion that the answer to all the questions was a big resounding NO.

CHAPTER 39

MARTIN

The garden was a jungle. He had never done much gardening; that had always been Fran's department. Martin put all his weight onto the spade and dug over another piece of flowerbed next to the patio. He could just imagine his wife's face on catching sight of her precious garden, left for far too long to run wild over the spring and early summer.

The tilling of the earth and the resultant weed-free bed was somehow satisfying, and he began to enjoy the exercise. As he dug he pondered on the best way of winning his wife back. She had been friendly enough when he had called round or they had met up at family functions, but so far she had shown no inclination to return home. Martin sighed and sweated, dug another clod of earth, and threw a stone at a cat squatting in a distant flower bed.

"Bugger off, you little bastard!"

The sun beat down upon his back, and Martin ignored aches and pains creeping around his body from the unaccustomed toiling, passing them off as retribution for his shortcomings. The more his muscles screamed, the harder he dug. Within a few hours all the flowerbeds were pristine, and his anger had dissipated somewhat.

He kicked the spade away and stretched his arms up to the sky. He thought of Colin at home with his family, and of Richard, loved-up and about to be married. A cloud of envy enveloped him. Tired and hungry but reluctant to heat up another meal for one, he started off towards the shed, pulled out the lawn mower from its moorings and filled it up with petrol. It roared into life straight away. The slow meander up and down the lawn cooled him, and each swathe he made through the foot long grass reinforced his determination to turn his life around once and for all.

***

"Hi, I'm Martin, and for forty years I've been a sex addict."

The applause seemed incongruous to him, but nevertheless he forced a smile. A younger man dressed casually in jeans and a bomber jacket spoke quietly as the group looked on with interest.

"Welcome, Martin. We're so glad you have joined us tonight. We meet three times a week; Monday, Wednesday and Friday evenings. I'm James, and everyone else will introduce themselves in a moment. At one time or another all of us here have been in the same boat. We are here to help each other. You've taken the first step towards recovery already, in admitting that you have a problem."

"Cheers." Martin sighed. "If it helps me to get my wife back then I'm all for it."

"Hi Martin." A balding man in his sixties leaned forwards in his seat. "I'm Charlie. My wife divorced me, but I ditched the porn and am taking it one day at a time. Who knows? I might even find a new lady!"

Martin grinned ruefully.

"Hey, let's hope so Charlie."

"Hi, I'm Dave." An overweight man in his forties stood up briefly to shake Martin's hand. "My marriage is improving finally, so don't give up."

"I'll try not to." Martin clasped Dave's hand firmly. "Everything's a bit shitty now, but as Frances often reminds me, it's all my own fault."

"I never realised I was addicted." Dave shook his head. "It's easy to get sucked in."

"*Too* easy. Hi, I'm Bob." A man Martin's age gave him a wave. "It seemed everybody knew about my porn addiction except me."

The group continued to look at him expectantly, but Martin felt himself relaxing slightly after the introductions. The first hurdle was over.

"Well, yeah, it took a bit of courage to join in tonight, but I'm glad I came along. I've been addicted to alcohol too in the past as well as porn, and never really thought about the effect it would have on my marriage. As far as I was concerned it was my little secret, a way of chilling out I suppose. I realised I made a big mistake when I wanted Frances to act out what I was watching on the screen."

Martin heard a few murmurs of assent, accompanied by some nods.

"My wife told me over and over again that I had a porn addiction, but I never listened to her." James shrugged. "Did you know it's the worst addiction to try and recover from?"

"No." Martin looked at James with surprise. "I didn't know that."

"Yeah." James replied. "Booze and drugs make you feel ill, but the porn, well, that one makes you feel good as you know."

"I'm nearly sixty years old." Martin sighed. "And I still have a lot to learn."

"You never stop learning, mate." Dave grinned. "Welcome to the club."

"Newbies get to make the tea." Bob interjected. "I'm glad to be able to pass *that* one on."

"No bar then?" Martin gave Bob a wink.

"Best not, eh?" Bob rolled his eyes to the ceiling. "Two sugars in mine please."

"Sugar addiction as well?" Martin began to enjoy himself. "Don't think I've had that one yet."

"Just give it time." Bob leaned back in his chair and laughed. "You'll get there."

***

He began to look forward to the meetings, and to enjoy the banter and male camaraderie. After sending a text message to Frances to let her know he had joined a support group, he waited for her reply, which failed to arrive. After a few weeks of waiting in vain Martin threw himself wholeheartedly into the group, liking the fact that while he was at a meeting, thoughts of his wife and what she was doing could mostly be put to the back of his mind. He had tried his best but had failed to win her back, and over a period of time arrived at the realisation that he needed to move forward with his life. He probably had another 20 or 30 years left, and it was time to start living again.

CHAPTER 40

FRANCES

She peeped out of the window in relief; her son's wedding day had dawned bright and clear. Frances checked her phone for any messages, but there were none. She felt a small frisson of disappointment; *was she to go by herself to the church? Why hadn't Martin got in touch about the travel arrangements?* What with all the baby paraphernalia in Colin and Jane's car, she knew there would be no room for her if she asked to go with them.

Frances soaked in the bath, took extra care with her make up, and dressed herself in the new pale blue suit she had been saving since the summer. By ten o'clock she was ready for the day. She picked up her phone and checked it once again, before dialling the number she knew so well.

"Hi."

She thought her husband sounded flat and disinterested. Slightly perturbed at the unusual response after weeks of silence, she put on her bubbliest telephone voice.

"Hey, it's only me. How's it going?"

"Great, thanks. How about you?"

She wanted to scream, but somehow kept it all together.

"What's happening about getting to the church?"

"No idea. I'll be going in the van though. The car's having some work done on it. What about you?"

Her dream of arriving to face the family in Martin's black BMW dissipated into the October air.

"Do you want a lift? I can drive round and pick you up if you like."

"Up to you really. The van's okay though."

"You can't turn up in that old van. I'll come by in half an hour. The boys will like it if we turn up together."

"Whatever you like. See you soon then."

Her annoyance deepened as she ended the call. *What mindfuckery was he up to now?* Frances grabbed her handbag and keys, and walked down the stairs to the communal hallway. Malcolm's front door opened.

"Hope it goes well, Fran. You look really nice."

"Cheers Malcolm. The weather's holding up at least."

She had not been to the house for months. As she brought the car to a halt outside her former home, Frances wondered whether she should use her key or ring the doorbell. She noticed with approval how the front garden had changed from a jumble of nettles to several neat flower beds as she walked down the path. By the time she reached the front door it was already open, with Martin standing there watching her.

"The garden looks lovely. I don't think I've ever seen it so weed free."

He smiled.

"You should see the back. I've laid a new patio as well. You look nice, by the way."

"Thanks." She returned the smile. "You've scrubbed up pretty good yourself."

It seemed strange walking into the hallway, which had obviously been painted since her departure. Her coat hook was still empty, while all of his outer garments had been thrown onto the second hook as usual.

"You've been busy." She looked around her. "I like the new colour scheme."

"Decorating keeps me busy, in between going to group meetings."

"Yeah, I got your text about that. How's it going?"

"Great." He kept his face deadpan. "If you're struggling with porn in the middle of the night, you can just ring one of the other guys and they'll bring round a new DVD that you haven't seen before."

She couldn't help but laugh at him.

"Seriously though, is it helping?"

"Sure is." He nodded. "I'm porn free. Have been for months actually."

"Glad to hear it. Shall we go to our son's wedding then?"

"Why not?" He took her arm. "Allow me to escort you to your car."

"I got here okay all on my own actually."

"Good for you." He steered her out of the door and locked it behind them. "*And* you always have the satnav in boy mode."

"Yeah." Frances giggled. "I'm a real ball breaker."

As she drove she enjoyed sharpening her wits on the banter running back and forth between them, and noticed glances of interest from friends and family as she parked up opposite the church.

"Look at your sister." Frances pointed to a middle-aged lady in a purple dress. "She's just dying to ask whether we're back together."

"Let her think what she likes." Martin shrugged. "We're okay with our situation, and so that's good enough for me."

Together she thought they made a united front as they walked arm in arm across the road to the churchyard. However, she felt something had changed in her husband, and as soon as they had greeted Richard, standing nervously by the main door, she realised what it was that had been bothering her. Martin, to all intents and purposes, seemed to have given up entirely on the possibility of her ever returning to the marital home.

***

Had it really been almost thirty six years since she had stood at the altar gazing up at her new husband the way that Lisa was now looking at Richard? Frances wiped a few tears away and concentrated on finding the next hymn as the organist began playing. The pristine gold band on her new daughter-in-law's finger sparkled in the fingers of light filtering in through an oval stained glass window. Beside her Martin sang lustily, unconcerned and enjoying the day. She thought back to the naïve girl she had been on her own wedding day, unformed and unaware that the man she had married was not all he appeared to be. Instead of joining in the chorus she asked herself the question once again; *is it really possible to know somebody inside out?* Frances sighed and hoped that for Lisa's sake Richard had not inherited his father's addictive nature.

She smiled at her son's new father-in-law as she took his arm to walk behind Richard, Lisa and the bridesmaids back up the aisle towards the photographer. In front of her Martin and the mother-of-the-bride had linked arms and were smiling benignly as they passed by the seated wedding guests. Frances thought of her broken marriage and her lost hopes and dreams, and felt she could cry a river of tears.

CHAPTER 41

MARTIN

Perched on top of a ladder with a brush in his hand, he felt his phone buzz in his pocket. Martin carried on painting for another half an hour until a continual buzz warned him of an incoming call. He placed his brush down carefully on the lid of the paint pot and reached into his overalls pocket, giving a little smile at the number on the display screen.

"Hey Fran, how's it going?"

"Great thanks. What are you up to?"

"I'm painting the ceiling in the front room and then I'm going to start on the walls. How about you?"

He detected a slight hesitation in her reply.

"Oh, nothing much. I've got a day off today, so I'm just catching up with you after the wedding really. Is your car working okay now?"

"Seems to be." He shifted uncomfortably on the ladder. "I can't really talk now, but you'll have to come and see the new look when I've finished."

"Oh…sure." He heard her laugh at the other end. "What colour is the new wallpaper?"

"No paper; a mate's plastered the walls, and then I'm painting them pale green. Wallpaper's old fashioned."

"Get you! Let me know when it's done and I'll come and give it the once over."

"Yeah, sure." He replied. "Next weekend I expect."

"Okay."

He whistled as he put the phone back in his pocket.

***

There wasn't a nook or cranny in the house that had escaped a makeover. As Martin climbed stiffly down the ladder clutching an empty can of paint, a tapping sound made him turn towards the window. In the front garden, his wife with her nose pressed up against the glass, was peering through the net curtains. He waved at her, turned off the radio, and made his way to the front door. He was greeted with a smile, which to him appeared surprisingly genuine.

"I tried ringing, but the music was too loud. Did you know you can hear it in the street?"

Martin shrugged.

"Not any more. I've turned it off. Haven't you got a key? You should have come in."

"I didn't like to. I just wanted to see the new decorating."

"Have a wander round. I've done every room over the past few months."

He went into the kitchen, washed his hands and switched on the kettle, while hearing her moving about upstairs. On opening the fridge door he gave a *tut* of annoyance as she walked into the room behind him.

"It'll have to be black coffee. I forgot to get any milk."

"That's okay." She laughed. "I don't mind."

"So…" He reached in the cupboard for two mugs. "What d'you think?"

"It all looks great." She nodded. "I'm impressed."

"No work then?"

The kettle boiled, and he made their drinks and handed her a mug. Frances shook her head and sat down on a breakfast bar stool.

"Not today, just evening classes tonight. Health and Social Care."

"What's that?"

"I learn how to wash bums properly, although I seemed to manage okay with Colin and Richard."

He laughed, sat down beside her, and took a sip of coffee.

"You can always practise on mine if you've forgotten."

Frances screwed up her nose.

"Only if you get dementia and end up at Sunset."

"Nice to know I'll have clean bits if I do." He raised a thumb. "So you'll get a degree in arse washing?"

He could tell she was enjoying the banter.

"Other things too, but a diploma, not a degree."

"Cool. On another note, I would have offered you a biscuit but I ate the last one this morning."

"How noble of you."

"Well, it looked lonely sitting in the tin on its own."

"You ought to go shopping more often."

"Yeah, that's what my mum said."

At the mention of her mother-in-law, Frances pulled a face.

"How is the old girl? Am I forgiven yet?"

"She keeps out of it. Anyway, I gave you good cause to go."

"You did." Frances nodded. "Still going to the group therapy thing?"

"Twice a week, yeah." Martin drained his cup. "I never realised I had an addiction, Fran. It took you walking out to tell me that."

He noticed she could barely conceal her surprise at his words. He shrugged his shoulders in a kind of resigned despair, and gave a wry chuckle.

"I'm a changed man, but it's too late now."

When her hand came to rest on his, he made no move to push it away.

"We can still be friends." She looked at him earnestly. "The boys would like that."

"So would I." Martin nodded. "Yes, so would I."

CHAPTER 42

FRANCES

She hated what he'd done to the front room, but she was enjoying spending more time in the house that had held so many memories. It was no trouble to fill up his fridge once a week, and in return he paid for her groceries. The lottery money was holding steady, and Frances felt that she had the best of both worlds. On the evenings when her dinner for one had lost its appeal, he would be there with a takeaway. As far as she could tell, they were getting on better than they had done in a long, long time.

On a Friday evening in early December Frances decided to spring a surprise. Evening classes had finished for Christmas, and so instead of letting herself out after filling up the fridge, she imagined the appreciation which would ensue on Martin returning home to find that she had prepared his favourite liver and bacon casserole.

It seemed strange to be cooking in her old kitchen with all the well-used saucepans and plates. The new lino and colour scheme was not to her liking and the general cleanliness was not up to her standards, but she felt happy to be in familiar territory as she pottered about.

Towards seven o'clock she heard Martin's van pull up on the

driveway. Frances switched off the oven and lifted out the casserole, placing it on a cork mat in front of their place settings. Thinking it strange that he was talking to himself as he turned the key in the lock, she went into the hallway.

"Oh!"

She stared blankly at the unknown woman standing next to her husband, who gazed back at her, equally perplexed. She heard Martin's voice emanating from somewhere seemingly far off.

"Fran! I didn't know you were coming over!"

She turned her head in slow motion towards him.

"Oh, don't worry, I'm off now. Enjoy your evening."

All she wanted to do was get away as fast as she could. She ran back to the table to grab her bag and coat, and pushed past the woman who was now standing in front of her in the kitchen doorway.

"Excuse me."

Her heart was pounding as she reached the car in seconds flat. Tears dropped onto her lap as she drove away, fearing the death knell for their marriage had been sounded. Frances reached Jade Gardens but did not remember driving there. As she stepped into the communal hallway the usual aroma of boiled vegetables suddenly made her want to gag.

***

Within a short space of time her life had seemingly been reduced to work, eat and sleep. Frances had heard nothing from Martin, and the boys were cagey when they visited, changing the subject if she probed too much. Since the embarrassment with the liver and bacon casserole, she had not been near nor by her old house. As she sat down to watch TV with her meal for one, Frances admitted to herself for the first time that she *was* lonely, and that living on her own was not all that it was cracked up to be. She was missing the companionship she'd had on the cruise, and *yes,* she *was* missing her husband after thirty five years together. Stupidly she had acted too soon, and had not given him a chance to control his addiction. Now he probably *had* nailed it, but somebody else was reaping the benefits.

The TV adverts were full of happy families eating succulent festive fare or loved-up couples giving each other presents. Frances could see no point in putting up a Christmas tree just for herself, and knew her sons would be busy with their own families on the big day itself. Colin now had two young children to keep him busy, and Richard was still wallowing in post-nuptial bliss; she'd had no invites from either of them. She decided there was only one thing for it; she would offer her services to Bernie at the homeless shelter. He was irritating to the nth degree, but anything was better than spending Christmas Day on her own.

She washed up her plate and cutlery, feeling soft curling tendrils of depression seeping over her. *Why was she not happy that she had got what she wanted?* She was living a stress-free life on her own, no longer needing to be a porn detective. *Life was grand, wasn't it?* As she put the plate away she sighed with the realisation that if she had only hung on for a while longer, then she could have finally lived with the man she thought she had married in the first place.

Just one box of 20 Christmas cards was enough this year. She turned off the TV and leafed through her address book, putting a line through all Martin's friends and relatives. She was on her own now, and no longer a young woman. Frances thought of all the lonely years ahead of her. Who would want her if she was pushing sixty? Did she want to start dating all over again with men who had been through divorces and were carrying sacks of emotional baggage? She came to the conclusion that again, the answer was a big resounding *NO.* She knew what she wanted, but it was too late. Martin had found somebody else. She had driven him away and would never get him back. It was all her own fault.

CHAPTER 43

MARTIN

When he woke up, his leg was still draped over Janet's warm naked body. Martin curled an arm around her middle, and rubbed his nose in the back of her neck. A mumble came from under the sheet.

"Bugger off…I'm still asleep."

He grinned, yawned, and closed his eyes again.

"What a shame."

"I get the feeling that's all you want me for."

When he awoke again he was alone, but he could detect an aroma of frying bacon wafting up the stairs. He turned over on his back and considered her last sentence before sleep had overcome him. *Did he love her as he had once loved Frances?* He sat on the side of the bed and ran his hands through his hair, already knowing the answer.

She must have been wearing his dressing gown, as it had disappeared from the hook behind the bedroom door. Martin donned a tee shirt and a pair of boxer shorts and sauntered down to the kitchen. He smiled at Janet as she turned away from the cooker to face him.

"Is she still filling up your fridge?" Janet waved a spatula in the air. "The bacon will soon be out of date, so I reckoned I'd better cook it."

"No, I have to get my own shopping now; what a bloody nightmare."

He sat down at the table, enjoying the unexpected early morning company.

"When's Twat back?"

She laughed as she expertly lifted sizzling rashers of bacon onto a plate and popped four slices of bread into the toaster.

"For your information *Matt* will be gone all week. Lucky me, eh?"

"Lucky *me*, more like." He leaned over the table to playfully slap her buttocks. "Fancy filling up my fridge?"

She chuckled as her derriere waggled suggestively beneath the thin material of his dressing gown.

"Just let me eat my sandwich first, and stick the kettle on instead of looking at my arse."

The smell of warm toast combined with the fried bacon started to make his mouth water. Martin prepared two cups of coffee and then went over to stand behind Janet as she buttered the toast, wrapping his arms around her waist.

"Move in with me; you know you want to."

"We'd hate each other after even a week." She shook her head and wriggled out of his embrace, carrying two plates of food to the table. "Besides, you know how it is."

"Yeah." Martin sat down opposite her. "You spend all his money and he's out with his toy boys."

"It suits us." Janet shrugged. "I make him look respectable and he gives me everything I want."

"Except sex."

"Yeah, but that's where *you* come in."

"So you just want me for my body?" Martin raised an eyebrow and took a huge bite of his sandwich.

"And your bacon." Janet laughed. "How about you? Has your wife gone for good?"

"Yeah, I think so." Martin squirted tomato sauce between the slices of toast. "I haven't heard from her for ages, but we haven't discussed divorce yet. I've given up trying to get her back. She'll return if and when she wants to I imagine."

"Silly cow." Janet took a sip of coffee. "A bit of porn never did anybody any harm."

"She's just not that way inclined." Martin shrugged. "I guess you can't have it all ways."

"You can in a minute." Janet gave him a leery grin.

***

The sheets had been in the washing machine twice, and they still held an essence of Janet's perfume. Martin fought off a twinge of annoyance as he made the bed up for the second time that day. The cloying scent was playing havoc with his sinuses, and somehow even though they were separated he still felt disloyal to Frances for bringing another woman into the house they had shared.

The solution came to him as he lay awake tossing and turning into the early hours. The answer was easy; the mortgage was paid, he would rent the house out to tenants and find somewhere to rent for himself! There would be no memories of Frances in the new property, and he could begin again, maybe even get the divorce rolling if she agreed. Martin wondered how counsellors got away with talking such bollocks and charging the earth for their time into the bargain. He eventually fell asleep convinced that a brand new start would be the key to a happier life for both of them.

***

He was surprised at how quickly she rang his doorbell after he had sent her a text. There were dark circles under her eyes, and he thought she had lost some weight. He gave her a smile as he ushered her into the front room.

"Thanks for coming round. I haven't seen much of you lately."

"Didn't want to impose." Frances sat down and looked at him. "Especially now you have a new lady friend."

"Oh, that's only Janet." Martin shrugged. "She's married, but I don't like living like a monk."

"I see". A faint smile crossed Frances' features. "Is she the one with the three garages?"

"Yeah."

He thought she seemed somewhat relieved, and so ventured forth with his plan.

"I'm thinking of renting out the house and moving into something like you've got. Also what do you think about a divorce? I'll take the blame, after all it's been my fault that you left in the first place. We're still young enough to find somebody else. It seems pointless going on like this."

He quickly checked her expression, which did not change. However, her voice gave her emotions away, which was husky and had a distinct quiver when she spoke.

"Whatever you want, Martin. I've caused you enough trouble. We were never sexually compatible. Now I'm going through the menopause and I don't think I ever want sex again to be honest, just companionship. One man has been plenty for me, let alone finding another one."

He felt saddened by her words, and at a loss for what to say next. Instead, he moved over to sit next to her on the sofa, putting an arm around her shoulders and giving her a little squeeze as he sat down.

"What can I say, Fran? We were happy though, before the porn set in, weren't we? I still love you, for God's sake. It's all a bloody mess."

He felt her shoulders convulse with sobs, and he held her close.

"So sorry, Fran, for everything."

When she had regained her composure she wiped her eyes and looked at him.

"I'll see a solicitor tomorrow and get the ball rolling. I'm sorry too; sorry that I could never give you what you wanted. It took thirty five years for me to realise I'd married the wrong person, but that's life and you only get one chance at it. You need to find a lady who loves you. I still care for you, but it's not enough."

She stood up and looked down at him, hunched in resignation.

"I'll see myself out; I know where the door is."

CHAPTER 44

FRANCES

Deana waved at her from behind the open office door.

"Fran! Come in!"

Frances gave Deana a smile and walked through onto the slightly threadbare carpet, closing the door behind her.

"I just wanted to congratulate you on obtaining your diploma." Deana pointed to an empty chair. "Do take the weight off your feet for a moment."

"Thanks." Frances sank down onto a seat. "It's been a busy morning."

"As you know, the only other carer who has a diploma is Bernie, but he's never wanted promotion. Therefore I'm offering you the temporary post of Assistant Manager, which will be more office based during the day, and may be made permanent. Would you be interested? It'll be more to do with organising the off-duty rotas, taking some of the work from me, and ordering food and other supplies, things like that. You'll still be hands on at the sharp end though to cover for holidays or if we're short staffed."

"Oh!" Frances could not resist a grin. "Of course, I'd love it!"

"I'm going to be taking a six month secondment. I'll be based at the hospital two days a week with the tissue viability team. I'll still be about, but obviously will need a bit of help here in the office."

"I can't wait to start!" Frances beamed at Deana. "Thanks for this."

Deana reached forward to shake Frances' hand.

"You're welcome. It might take you a while to get your head around the rotas though, especially if you have a lot of distractions at home."

"Oh no, I'm divorced now." Frances shrugged. "I live alone."

Deana smiled and waved an arm about expansively.

"Welcome to the madhouse."

***

Her life on a day to day basis went on in a kind of agreeable routine. There were no particular highlights or low points, but she was happy in her work and if she lacked companionship her three grandchildren were always there to spoil. She had offered her services as a babysitter to both Colin and Richard, and had been amply rewarded. She felt close to all three grandchildren, and as far as she was concerned it gave her something to do in the evenings. Charlie and Frankie were lively boys who kept her on her toes, but if she had to pick a favourite, Frances knew it would have been Celia, Richard and Lisa's three month old daughter. The beautiful doe-eyed baby was placid and content, and Frances enjoyed sitting Celia in the crook of her arm all evening, even though she knew Lisa preferred the baby to go to sleep in her cot with its special bamboo safety mattress.

On one such evening after Celia had finished a bottle of milk, Frances carried the baby into the front room, put a clean nappy on her, and settled down with Celia under one arm to watch TV. All around the room were family photos that Lisa had lovingly enclosed in matching frames. One such photo usually caught Frances' eye; a recent one of Martin sitting just where she was on the sofa, and cuddling Celia close to him. His hair had greyed completely, and to Frances he looked considerably older. She kissed the top of Celia's head, and it occurred to her that the baby had the same shaped nose as Richard and her ex-husband. She looked at Martin's open expression and wondered just what was going on behind his eyes. *Was he still using porn?* She sighed and came to the swift conclusion that it was now none of her business; she would never know, and therein was the eternal problem that would always be between them until the end of her days.

Was she a prude? Did other women with the same problem just ignore it instead of divorcing their husbands? As she held Celia close to her and rocked her gently to and fro, it occurred to her that maybe *she* had been addicted too; not to porn, but to searching for it. *Could she trust any man not to have a stash of adult movies hidden away? What about Bernie? What about Colin and Richard? Were they addicted? Why was her life still being ruled by porn, even though she and Martin were divorced?* Frances looked down at her granddaughter, and had a sudden urge to keep Celia innocent for as long as possible, free from the seedy world of sex. She wanted to lock her away in an ivory tower. She whispered to Celia that there were no Prince Charmings in the world, just testosterone-fuelled men eager to use women for their own sexual gratification. The lure of the big white wedding dress and gold band duped young girls unaware of the male psyche into a kind of happy-ever-after Never-Never land. She had long ago figured out there had seldom been a heterosexual man born upon the earth who did not want a return in the bedroom for promising to love, honour and cherish at the altar. The baby gazed back at her with wise old-before-time eyes. Frances had the eerie feeling that Celia could understand every single word she said.

CHAPTER 45

MARTIN

He turned off the back-up computer, switched the wires back to his normal hard drive, and zipped up his fly. A little bit of porn in the mornings before setting off for work was certain to put him in a good mood for the rest of the day, and Martin was smiling. It was a harmless release of tension, despite all the past furore over his so-called addiction that his ex-wife had stirred up. He was his own man now, and free to do as he pleased, so why not indulge his whims when he felt like it? A few beers while watching porn, and then sex with whoever he could find after work was infinitely preferable to listening to a group of tossers trying to talk him out of it. Martin reasoned they were all probably secretly using the same adult sites as he was when they were on their own anyway.

The van started first time, further augmenting his good mood. As he pulled away from the kerb, Martin glanced to his left and sure enough a net curtain was twitching in the flat below. He had seen her about a couple of times, a forty-something woman with unremarkable features and unrealistically blonde hair. He raised his arm in salutation and a dark shadow disappeared from behind the window.

The A140 was busy into Norwich, with nose to tail traffic. He reached into the glove compartment, grabbed a disc from the top of the pile, and fed it into the upmarket DVD player he had installed himself at great expense. As far as he was concerned, why should he try and fight the traffic when he could indulge himself for a little while longer?

***

It had been a good day, and the job had gone well. Martin slid the van into his allotted parking spot and turned off the engine. He yawned and opened the driver's door, making a mental note to write down the number of the new Chinese takeaway pinned to the notice board in the communal hallway.

As he turned his key in the main lock and opened the front door he could see the door to the garden was open at the other end of the passage. The forty-something woman grinned at him as she came up the steps carrying an overloaded laundry basket.

"Hi. At last the rain held off long enough!"

Martin smiled and thought she looked better close up, and was certainly an improvement on the miserable old git who had lived there before.

"Ah, you're the new tenant in the ground floor flat? I'm Martin Andrews, I live upstairs."

"Pleased to meet you Martin. Yeah, I moved in last week. I'm Rachel East. I'm just about straight now in the flat thank goodness. Come in for a cup of tea if you like?"

"Why not?" Martin made his voice sound as casual as possible. "Cheers."

He had never been into the flat when the old man lived there. Martin noticed all the walls looked freshly painted. There was a distinct lack of family photos in the living room as he sat down on the settee and looked around, but he approved of the functional furniture and lack of clutter.

"You've been busy." He nodded approvingly. "Nice room."

"Thanks." Rachel took out a couple of coasters from their stand on the coffee table. "Tea? Milk and sugar?"

"Yeah, ta. Two sugars." Martin noticed the coasters were imprinted with a picture of a smiling Rachel sitting next to another forty-something woman with short dark hair.

"That's different from your face being on the tea towels." He chuckled.

"My late partner Chris." Rachel picked up a coaster and gazed at it wistfully. "She died a couple of years ago. Somebody had them printed for me. I don't really care for loads of photos hanging about, but I do like these. Anyway, I'll be back in a minute with some tea, so make yourself comfortable."

He masked a stab of disappointment and took the opportunity to make another sweep of the room in her absence. A large black cat slunk into the room and jumped on his lap. He stroked the soft fur and felt the creature purring under his fingers.

"You've found Moose." Rachel came back in carrying a tray. "He seems to like you."

"He found *me* actually." Martin laughed. "I was just sitting here minding my own business."

He took a cup of tea from Rachel, who sat down opposite and passed him a plate of biscuits."

"Have you lived here long?"

"About a year." Martin took a hob-nob. "It took a while to find the right tenants for my house after my divorce."

"Oh, sorry." Rachel made a face. "Didn't mean to pry."

He shrugged.

"It's okay. I was an arsehole; still am probably, if you ask Fran.

We meet up at family functions. It's all very civilised. I'll see Fran at our granddaughter's christening on Sunday. Sometimes she even rings me up for a chat."

"I was with Chris for twenty years." Rachel sighed. "Living on your own can be hard sometimes, can't it?"

Martin nodded, unwilling to divulge any more information. As far as he was concerned he had said enough already.

***

"I baptise you in the name of the Father, and of the Son, and of the Holy Spirit."

As the vicar sprinkled holy water over her, Celia woke up and gave it her all. Martin already had a headache, and he whispered to Frances next to him in the pew.

"D'you still keep paracetamols in your bag?"

She passed him a tablet and he swallowed it whole. The baby's shrill protestations fought tooth and nail with his tinnitus, and Martin closed his eyes.

"Don't go to sleep like you did at Charlie's christening."

Her voice in his ear made him smile, as he turned and whispered a reply.

"I wasn't asleep, I was inspecting the inside of my eyelids."

When the service was over he was relieved to escape the musty smell of the church and pose with the family outside for the photo-shoot in the fresh air. He savoured a brief feeling of belonging as he stood next to Frances, who was holding a now sleeping Celia.

"It's my birthday next week. Fancy seeing a West End show to celebrate?" He held his breath and silently debated how to deal with her refusal.

"Okay." She replied without hesitation and smiled at the camera. "Which one?"

"I think there's a good musical on at the Savoy Theatre. Cheers for that."

He grinned broadly as she passed the baby to him.

"You're welcome Grandad. It'll make a change from working at the shelter."

He looked down at his granddaughter's perfect little features and knew he would kill any man who touched even one hair on her head.

"I'll drive up. We can leave the car in Parker Mews and walk down the Strand. Maybe even grab a bite to eat?"

"Now you're pushing it." She laughed. "Just as long as it's not curry though."

"Done."

He felt unaccountably happy as he reluctantly passed Celia back to her mother.

CHAPTER 46

FRANCES

She smiled at herself in the mirror, pleased with her final choice. Around her on the floor lay several dresses and suits, each one discarded at the last moment. Frances fastened the top button of a cream-coloured jacket and swivelled the matching skirt around to hang correctly on her waist. The skirt had been too small the previous year, and her slight weight loss had been beneficial.

She tied a vermilion chiffon scarf at a jaunty angle, and slipped into a pair of burgundy suede court shoes. With just a touch of makeup and a last brush of her newly highlighted hair which shone under the bathroom spotlights, she considered herself ready for a night on the town. Frances made a mad dash into the bedroom with armfuls of clothes just as the doorbell rang. She grabbed her bag and keys and unused to shoes with heels, made her way carefully down to the communal hall and opened the door.

"Bloody hell!" Martin took a step back. "You look great!"

"Happy birthday." She beamed at him. "I've got a little present in my bag for you. You can open it now or later if you want."

"I'll open it in the car before we start off."

They strolled side by side down the path towards the car. She felt strangely excited.

"What did the boys buy you?"

"Colin and Jane gave me one of those Buyagift thingies. I'm going hot air ballooning." He chuckled. "I'm bloody terrified! Richard said he didn't have a lot of money so he bought me a basin wrench. He knew I needed one to change the bathroom sink."

She laughed and gave a little curtsey as he opened the passenger door.

"This is the second time you've opened the door for me. I'm getting worried."

He bowed stiffly.

"The answer's the same as before. It's the new me."

She reached in her bag and brought out a small parcel as he moved to the other side of the car and opened the driver's door.

"Here you are; hope you like it."

He took the present from her and eyed it with interest as he made himself comfortable and started up the engine.

"Cheers Fran. I can't say I'm over the moon about being sixty, but if it means I get to go out with you, then it can't be too bad."

He ripped open the paper and smiled. Frances chuckled.

"I didn't know what to get you. I liked that photo of you and Celia at Richard's place."

"It's great." He twisted the mug around in his hands. "*You're* missing on it though."

"You don't want my mug on your mug." She laughed. "It might crack."

"You're beautiful, Fran. Always were and always will be."

She looked out of the side window as he pulled away from the kerb, unwilling to see the longing in his eyes that his voice was failing to hide. Her mind was in turmoil. Had he really come to terms with his addictions? To her at that moment it seemed as though her ex-husband might have finally turned over a new leaf of his own volition. She needed to know, once and for all.

"How's the group therapy? Still going?"

She heard a snort emanating from her right.

"I don't need that anymore. I told you I'm a changed man, and it's all down to you. You made me see what porn had done to us. If I could turn back the clock to before it all went wrong, then I would."

As the A11 turned into the M11, a companionable silence settled over them. Frances noticed the indentation where a wedding band used to be on the third finger of Martin's left hand had all but disappeared.

"I thought you'd have found somebody else by now."

He put the car in cruise control and shrugged.

"I haven't met anyone who matches up to you. One talked so much shite I couldn't wait to get away. How about you? Still going about with that Bernie fella?"

"He's a friend, but not in *that* way. If you heard him eating a boiled sweet you'd know why."

He grinned and glanced to his left.

"It's not easy at our age… it's lonely, isn't it?"

She was aware he was scanning her features for confirmation. Frances sighed and nodded.

"It can be, sure, but work keeps me busy now I've been promoted."

She noticed the whites of his knuckles as he gripped the steering wheel a little harder than was necessary.

"I decorated the whole bloody house hoping you'd come back. When you didn't, I couldn't live there anymore so I stored our stuff and rented it out. The current tenants have another two months on their contract." He cleared his throat before carrying on. "D'you think you'll ever want to live with me again, Fran? We were married for so long. I still love you. We'll be seventy in ten years' time. Hell, we could be dead by then!"

She had known the question was coming. Frances sank back in her seat and a pregnant silence filled the car. She thought about the father of her children, about forgiveness, respect, and companionship in her old age. She cast her mind back to the years of being a porn detective; the lies, the secrecy, and the lack of trust. *Was it possible for a man to kick the most pleasurable addiction of all? Could she believe he had changed after decades of watching other people having sex?* She still had no idea, but it was time to look out for Number One. Living alone wasn't all that it was cracked up to be. She was lonely, and the thought of living with somebody who loved her rather than nobody at all was suddenly more appealing after two years on her own. *Did she love him?* She couldn't answer that one, but they had known each other for nearly forty years, and now they shared two sons, two daughters-in-law, and three grandchildren. He would always be there as part of the family.

"No porn?" She looked at him.

"Not even a nipple." He grinned at her.

"I'll think about it." She shrugged. "That's all I can do."

"That's good enough for me." He nodded. "Take your time."

***

She did not resist when he took her hand as they left Parker Mews and walked along Drury Lane. All around them couples, gay or straight, strolled arm in arm and took in the sights of London. To be one half of a couple again felt strange to her, and if she was honest with herself, she was enjoying it. Just before the Strand Palace hotel she glanced down a side road and recognised a small figure encased in a sleeping bag propped up against a wall.

"That's Tony." She took a second look. "He goes to the shelter."

She stopped as Martin followed her gaze and then looked at his watch.

"I'll go back to Subway's, we've just passed one. I'll get him a sandwich." He replied. "The Strand Palace do a lovely carvery buffet. We can go there before the show."

She turned around, running to keep up with his long, loping strides.

"When have you ever bothered about homeless people before?" She panted.

"Since my halo got put back on straight." He opened the door to Subway's café. "It was a bit wonky before."

She stood outside on the street and waited for him, enjoying the sights and sounds of the city of her birth. Somebody waved to her from an open topped tourist bus and she raised her right arm in salutation.

"Who are you waving to?"

She looked around at Martin, who had appeared clutching the largest baguette she had ever seen, stuffed with every kind of meat, cheese and salad that Subway's could offer.

"I don't know who it was…good God, poor old Tony hasn't got many teeth, he'll have to gum it to death."

"My old mum always said if you're going to have one, have a big one." Martin looked at the baguette approvingly. "This is making my mouth water."

She liked the way he spent a few moments chatting to Tony as he handed over the baguette. She stood back and watched their interaction before walking towards them, disappointed to discover that Tony did not recognise her.

***

"Mmm…smoked salmon, my favourite."

Frances smiled at Martin and put a forkful of smooth fishy delight to her lips, enjoying the sight of her ex-husband tucking in to his prawn cocktail starter.

"I told you – it's a great buffet here; all you can eat." He nodded. "What's more, I'm paying, so it's all good."

Frances swallowed another mouthful of salmon.

"You're a prince."

"Thought you were going to say something else then." Martin gave her a sly look.

"Couple of years back yeah, I might have done." She chuckled.

He grimaced.

"Sorry I *was* such a prick." He sighed. "I don't blame you for going."

"All I wanted to do was to get away as fast as I could. Now I've been away I've seen both sides of the coin, so to speak." She speared another sliver of salmon. "It appears the grass *isn't* always greener on the other side."

She noticed him look up quickly at her statement.

"D'you like living on your own?" He put down his fork. "I don't, it's bloody awful."

She shrugged.

"It has its moments, but sure, it can be lonely."

He reached across the table and took her hand.

"We can be company for one another in our old house again if you like, and I'll get all our stuff out of storage. Separate bedrooms as well if that's what you want. No pressure. We know each other inside out, you *know* we do."

"That's what I'm afraid of!" Frances chuckled.

"I told you, there won't be any of that malarkey anymore." He sighed. "We don't have to be lonely in our old age, we'll have each other."

"Your tenants' contract runs out in two months?" She looked at him for confirmation.

"Yeah." He nodded. "Two months."

"I'll give you your answer before then."

"Cheers Fran." He squeezed her fingers. "At least you haven't said *no.*"

196

CHAPTER 47

Frances felt a twinge of annoyance as Mavis took the last biscuit from the tin and took a bite whilst fixing her with a questioning look.

"And he wants you to go back to him?"

"Yes." Frances nodded.

"All men are pervs." Syvia rolled her eyes heavenwards as she sipped her tea. "You should have lived with my ex."

"Not all of us." Bernie looked indignant. "Looks like it's down to me to stand up for one half of the human race."

"With the exception of *you*, Bernie." Sylvia chuckled. "Go on then, Fran, what's stopping you?"

Frances finished her tea and rinsed her cup under the tap while thinking up a suitable reply.

"He says he's changed, but I suppose I'll never know if he has or if he hasn't."

"So … you don't trust him?" Mavis put the lid back on the biscuit tin and stood up.

"I *want* to trust him." Frances sighed. "But I don't want to be let down again."

"Ooh….tricky." Mavis nodded. "I guess somewhere along the line maybe you have to forgive and let him have the benefit of the doubt."

"Never give a man the benefit of the doubt." Sylvia shook her head. "He'll shit on you at the first opportunity."

"Cheers you lot." Frances laughed. "What do you think, Bernie?"

"As a confirmed bachelor I'm staying out of it." Bernie held up one hand in supplication. "You're on your own there Fran."

"Go with your heart, Fran." Deana sent a text message and looked up from her phone. "It's the best judge of all."

"Yes." Frances agreed. "I think you're probably right."

"Don't give up your flat straight away if you go back to him." Sylvia held up a warning finger. "As they say, suck it and see…"

***

Deep in thought, Frances strolled out of Sunset and meandered along the high street in the direction of Jade Gardens. The late afternoon Spring sunshine held no warmth, and she shivered slightly in her padded coat and pulled it around her more securely. In front of her a businessman in an overcoat carried a briefcase in one hand, and a bunch of flowers in the other. She smiled and imagined the bouquet's recipient; a perfect wife with two perfectly behaved children, one boy and one girl. The boy helped his father with jobs around the house, and the girl helped her mother in the kitchen. Frances suppressed a snort of laughter and wondered not for the first time whether apart from children's reading books from the 1960's, a family such as that had ever existed. She quickly brought the book up to date in her head: *Daddy looks at porn, Mummy tries to find it, and Sally helps Mummy. Timmy finds Daddy's porn when he is at work, and thinks it's the best thing since sliced bread.*

Where had Daddy hidden the porn? That was the eternal question. Daddy had become so good at hiding it, that Mummy could search the house from top to bottom and still be none the wiser. She thought back to Sylvia's statement; *were* all men perverts? Frances had no idea. As she walked up the path to her front door to face her usual dinner-for-one she wondered for the millionth time whether she could at last trust her ex-husband, or whether moving in with him would cause her to once more become the reluctant porn detective she had never wanted to be.

***

She picked up her phone and started to compose a message:

'Hi Martin, I've made a decision. Let's try it for three months and see how it goes, but I'll keep my flat on just in case!'

She pressed 'send', and waited.

Fifteen minutes later she answered the doorbell and found herself immediately swung around and swept up in a bear hug.

"You've no idea how happy that text has made me!"

She looked up at her ex-husband, grinning from one ear to the other.

"Come upstairs!" She hissed. "Malcolm will be out in a minute to see what's going on!"

She felt him pat her behind lightly as he followed her up the stairs.

"Yes Ma'am! I'm right behind you!"

Safely back in her flat, Frances tried her best to dampen his spirits.

"It's just a trial run, Martin. I have to be sure we're not going to be playing the same old mind games again that we did last time."

"I told you, that's all over. I'm lonely, and you're lonely. You've made the right decision. We'll be great company for each other. The boys will be over the moon."

Frances felt like hugging him.

"I still want separate bedrooms though for that three months at least." She stated with some assertiveness. "I don't know if we'll ever get back to how we used to be, but I want to take it slowly."

"Of course." He nodded. "Take as much time as you want."

At that moment she knew he would give her whatever she wanted. Frances regarded her ex-husband's smiling face and considered how at last it might be time for her to learn to forgive, try to forget, and finally to do the third thing on Rhona's marriage repair list … move on.

CHAPTER 48

Slowly, and with great reverence, Frances closed Albert Tyler's eyes for the last time. Laying out the dead was now as natural to her as caring for the living. She removed the chin strap from the bed head just as Sylvia Dalton poked her head around the bedroom door.

"Poor old sod." Sylvia tutted. "All alone in the world; no rellies."

"I know." Frances sighed. "Isn't it sad? The council will have to bury him."

Sylvia moved further into the room and closed the door behind her.

"About our conversation in the staff room the other day." She whispered. "I really think you're making a big mistake moving back with your ex. I just can't stress that enough."

Frances smiled at her friend.

"I have to give him one last chance to redeem himself. Plus the fact I see old Albert here with nobody, and I don't want that for my old age."

"You've got your sons and grandchildren though." Sylvia walked up to the bed. "Albert never married."

Frances nodded.

"Yes, but they've got their own lives. I don't want to be a burden. Give us a hand with this plugging. You might as well, now you're here."

Together the two women worked silently on making Albert presentable for the undertaker. Frances waited for Sylvia to ask the question she knew her friend had been wanting to find out the answer to for some time. As they wrapped the old man in a sheet and tagged his toe, Sylvia drew a breath.

"So why *did* you leave him?"

Frances had often rehearsed a few bland words to leave a person none the wiser, but at that moment she felt a compulsion to rid herself of her problem once and for all.

"In a nutshell, he was addicted to porn. That led to him seeking out prostitutes, amongst other things, and it made me addicted to searching for it in the house – a porn detective you might say. Life became too stressful, and I left."

She felt so much better for telling somebody else, and saw Sylvia stand up straight and gaze at her with an open mouth.

"You're joking! That's exactly the reason why I left my own husband!"

Frances smiled at her friend in a brief moment of understanding. Sylvia went over to Frances and gave her a hug.

"He'll never stop, you know that don't you? He's addicted. There's no cure for it."

"He says he's done with it all." Frances shrugged. "I want to forgive him and start again."

"If he's got that addictive personality, then you're on a loser. My ex ended up on the sex offenders' register."

"Oh God." Frances sighed. "I don't want to know any more."

"It's grim, Fran. If they can be helped it might take years of therapy….*years*." Sylvia whispered. "Even then they can relapse at any time."

Frances washed her hands and composed herself.

"We're companions for each other. I don't want to be a lonely old lady. I'll never know if he *has* stopped looking at it, but I'm going to take his word for it. Life's hard enough let alone trying to live out your last years frail and with nobody around to help."

"You're young enough to find somebody else." Sylvia shook her head. "God, you're not even sixty yet."

Frances moved away from the sink and ran the tap for Sylvia.

"I don't want anybody else, Sylvie. I've known him since I was seventeen. We've got two sons and three grandchildren together. And who knows? I may end up with somebody even worse."

"True, true." Sylvia slapped some liquid soap onto her hands. "But you may get someone better."

"I don't want to take that risk. Being post-menopausal doesn't help either. Martin accepts I don't want a sexual relationship now."

"Forgive me if I'm being a bit thick here." Sylvia dried her hands. "But if he's a sex addict like you say, where do you think he's going to get his thrills from?"

Frances shrugged.

"I just don't want to think about that. He says he's stopped, and I believe him."

"On your head be it." Sylvia walked towards the door. "Has Deana got the green sheet?"

Frances nodded.

"Yes."

"Then I'll phone the undertakers."

Frances turned around to take one last look at the shrouded figure that had once been Albert Tyler. *Had Albert had a porn addiction?* She still did not know if it was normal or natural for men to spend hour after hour watching other people having sex. Had she made too much fuss over Martin's habit? *Was she a prude? Had the whole problem been her fault from the start? How could she turn her back on somebody she had known for over half her lifetime?*

She left Albert's room and quietly closed the door. Albert's life was over, but as far as she was concerned, she was doing her best to ensure that her own porn-free future was just beginning.

***

She had paid three months' rent in advance. As she packed her clothes into a suitcase she heard a tap on the door and Malcom's voice hissing through the letterbox.

"Fran! Is it true? Are you leaving us?"

She smiled and opened the front door.

"Come in Malcolm. Yes, I'm going back to my husband on Saturday, but I'm hedging my bets. I'm keeping the flat on for three months."

"You'll be back." Malcolm pointed a finger at her. "He's an arsehole."

"Cheers for that." Frances laughed. "We'll see."

"Emma told me, but she reckons you won't return." Malcolm smiled at her. "She's got rose-tinted glasses since the new boyfriend's appeared on the scene."

"Ah yes, just wait and see, Malcolm. I'll know after three months I think."

"I hope you come back." Malcolm shook her hand. "You deserve better than him."

Frances gave Malcolm a hug.

"Yes I spoke to Emma yesterday. She's happy for me, probably the only one who is."

"No, you go and live your life." Malcolm shook his head. "Take no notice of me. I hope it works out for you."

"Cheers." Frances grinned. "Me too."

CHAPTER 49

"Frances! Lovely to see you again! Do come in."

She followed Rhona along the passageway to her consulting room, and sat down on what she now termed 'her' side of the two seater sofa. Rhona poured herself a glass of water and sat back in the armchair opposite.

"How are things?"

"Okay." Frances nodded. "But I just wanted to come and see you. I've decided to go back and live with Martin. He assures me he's finished with porn for good."

"Great!" Rhona tapped a pen against her notepad. "So you've managed to build some trust between you now?"

"The holiday helped, as you knew it would. I saw another side of him on the cruise that I hadn't seen for a long time. He really wants us to make a go of it."

"I'm so glad the two of you are happier now. And you don't feel the need to check up on him?" Rhona regarded Frances inquisitively.

"After such a long time of *not* looking for porn, I've simply got out of the habit." Frances shrugged. "I think it *was* an addiction too. All I needed was to stop doing it for a while, and the compulsion went away."

"Absolutely." Rhona nodded. "Learned behaviours just need to be un-learned."

"So … what happens if I'm wrong and he's still addicted?" Frances voiced the fear that had been trying to make its way to the forefront of her brain for a while. "How will I know?"

"You'll know." Rhona smiled and crossed her legs. "You found out before, didn't you?"

"I don't want to start creeping around again when he's out, looking in every nook and cranny." Frances shook her head. "So I'm going to do that thing I could never do before… *trust* him."

"Well done." Rhona laughed. "I'm sure you'll both be very happy."

"It won't be through lack of trying on my part." Frances sighed. "Thanks for all your help."

Rhona reached forward and shook Frances' hand.

"My pleasure."

As Frances walked back down the passageway she realised with a wry smile that the counsellor had been very clever in *not* imparting any of her own opinions about their relationship. Whatever conclusion she had eventually come to, Frances felt proud that she had made that decision entirely on her own. She had *chosen* to trust Martin, and now she looked forward to unearthing the love for her ex-husband which had been hidden away within her for so many years. She had laid the first foundation stone of their new life together, and she felt *good*.

EPILOGUE

The last time she had slept in her old bedroom it had been as a married woman coming up to her ruby wedding anniversary. Frances' gaze trailed from her Kindle to the empty third finger on her left hand as she sat up in bed listening to the familiar creaking of hot water pipes cooling and the house settling down for the night. She switched off the side lamp, and underneath her bedroom door came a comforting glow of light emanating from Martin's room across the landing.

Had she done the right thing? Should she have listened to Sylvia? She had no idea, but she was enjoying the suffusion of feel-good endorphins from her new, forgiving nature. She was stress-free, and no longer felt compelled to tear the house apart looking for evidence of Martin's addictions; he had told her he no longer watched porn, and that was good enough for her. *Did she love him?* She still couldn't answer that one. She trusted him, had a companion for her old age, and did not feel alone or lonely. As far as she was concerned the love would return in time and anyway, it was *better the devil you know.* She lay back on the pillows and smiled. It was good to be home again. She closed her eyes and slept like a baby.

***

On the other side of the landing Martin turned up the iPhone's volume and adjusted his headphones for comfort just as the couple on the screen were coming to their climax. His heart beat faster as he silently masturbated to the couple's frantic rhythm, enjoying the sounds of sex and the discharge of tension upon reaching his own orgasm. When the short movie had finished, he wiped himself with a tissue, turned off the phone, and then lay back on the pillows and smiled. His wife, the love of his life, had returned to the fold, and he would do whatever it took to make her happy. However, he knew he could not live without the release that porn had always given him. As far as he was concerned it was a harmless escape from reality for a few moments; he had done it for more years than he could remember. Frances could not access passwords on his phone or on the back-up computer in his office. There would be nothing else for her to find.

Martin yawned. It was good to be home again. He closed his eyes and slept like a baby.

THE END

You may also like to read 'No Sex Please, I'm Menopausal!' also by Stevie Turner.